MY NAME IS BLADE

"I come in peace to the people of the Tower of the Serpent, from a distant land called England. I would speak with the rulers of the Tower of the Serpent."

"You are not of Melnon?" the warrior asked.

"What is Melnon?" queried Blade.

"Melnon is the world," the warrior said sharply. "You say that you come from Beyond. Or perhaps"—the warrior hesitated as if he were about to use obscene language—"one of the other towers has foresworn the War Wisdom of Melnon. They are sending men among the Waste Land at the foot of the Tower of the Serpent, to catch and kill the First on the Ground." Kir-Noz drew both swords and flourished them so that they whistled in the air. "The tower that forgot the War Wisdom of Melnon will pay in time. But you shall pay at once!" Without any further words the man sprang toward Blade.

The Blade Series

BLADE

THE TOWERS OF MELNON

by Jeffrey Lord

PINNACLE BOOKS • NEW YORK CITY

This is a work of fiction. All the characters and events portrayed in this book are fictional, and any resemblance to real people or incidents is purely coincidental.

BLADE: THE TOWERS OF MELNON

Copyright © 1975 by Lyle Kenyon Engel

An original Pinnacle Books edition, published for the first time anywhere.

ISBN: 0-523-00688-8

First printing, August 1975

Printed in the United States of America

PINNACLE BOOKS, INC.
275 Madison Avenue
New York, N.Y. 10016

BLADE
THE TOWERS OF MELNON

CHAPTER ONE

England is a small and crowded country. Enough vacant land for the type of training center the secret intelligence agency MI6 wanted to build is often hard to come by. MI6 wanted at least a square mile with buildings, which doesn't grow on bushes along every cowpath and byway.

But it so happened that, just as MI6's search was beginning, a certain earl was being buried. This earl had been at Eton with the man called J, the head of MI6, in the days before World War I. This was so long ago that neither of the men enjoyed being reminded of how long ago it had been. But the friendship had lasted down the years. It had lasted as J rose to be one of the most distinguished spymasters in the free world, and as the earl rose to be a general, complete with VC and DSO, and later became a distinguished member of Parliament. But no amount of distinction can ensure that a man will not fall from a horse and break his neck, and the earl did just that.

J attended the funeral at the earl's family seat. Afterwards the new earl ushered him into the great, gloomy, oak-paneled library. There he made J a proposition concerning the disposal of the family estate—or at least of part of it.

"You know what death duties are like, sir," said the younger man. "We should be able to hold on to the main estate. But father was rather old-fashioned. He preferred to keep as much in land as possible. We don't have much cash, so we're going to have to sell off the Herefordshire estate."

"Indeed?" said J, with deceptive placidity.

"Yes. It's not a great huge thing, less than fifteen hundred acres. And the house is a great wretched Victorian pile that sheds tiles and chimney pots on alternate Thursdays. But the stables are in good shape, and there's plenty of room. Also a good bit of privacy. The land's heavily wooded, and the walls and fences have been kept up fairly well. My father was a bit—ah, shirty, when it came to trespassers. Got in trouble with the county over that a few times."

"I know," said J. He had been a guest at this same estate a number of times before, during, and after World War II.

"The thing of it is," said the young earl, "I think father would have liked you to have a chance at the Herefordshire estate."

"Why me?" said J. His placidity was even more deceptive now.

"Well, he always said he thought you were in some sort of—well, secret intelligence work. MI5 or something like that. You know, James Bond stuff?"

"Suppose I were?" said J. "What does that have to do with the estate?"

"If you were, it occurred to father that you might want a training center of some sort. A nice secluded training center, someplace where a lot of tourists and passersby won't be butting in."

J nodded. He kept his professional poker face, so he did not light up like a Christmas tree with sheer delight. At least not on the outside. But he did take a deep breath before saying, "I see."

"We'd have to sell it," the young earl went on. "I doubt if the law would just let us donate it. But I'll see about keeping the price down as far as I can. I know the intelligence agencies aren't exactly rolling in money these days."

"Except in America," said J with a wry grin. The wealth of people and equipment that his American colleagues had was always a sore point with him, sometimes a major one. *They*

2

could claim at least a dozen estates of the size the young earl was offering.

"True," said the younger man. "But I think father would have wanted you to get it cheap. He was always very big on the patriotic type of stuff—doing your bit for England and all that sort of thing."

"Yes," said J in an even voice. "He was 'very big' on serving England. He risked his life doing it in two wars, as a matter of fact."

The young earl flushed slightly, recognizing a polite put-down when he heard one. To cover his embarrassment he went over to the sideboard and mixed two stiff Scotch-and-sodas. Then he returned to his chair and the two men got down to business.

Once they did, it was a simple matter of two phone calls to London—one apiece—and a few lines scribbled on a sheet of paper torn from the note pad next to the telephone. And MI6 found itself prospectively in possession of fifteen hundred acres of Herefordshire, at something less than ten pounds per acre.

After that, J went out to his Rover and put in two more calls on his scrambler-equipped radio-telephone. Both of these were also to London. One was to a man named Lord Leighton.

"Leighton, we've got the place for the new training center."

"Splendid work. Where?"

"Not even on a scrambled line, if you don't mind."

"Oh, to be sure, to be sure."

"I'm starting back to London in a few minutes. Can you meet me for lunch at my club? Tomorrow at noon?"

"Certainly."

"See you then."

The second call was to a man named Richard Blade.

"Richard, my boy. How are you?"

"Tolerably well, sir. Just got back from Scotland. Fishing, a little rock-climbing, you know."

"Fishing for what, Richard?" J knew that Blade was rather a woman-chaser, although he was always a gentleman about it. J neither approved nor disapproved.

"Salmon, sir. Nothing else," Blade replied with a hint of mock reproach in his voice.

"Very good, very good. Now—we've picked up a place to use for that training facility I mentioned."

"The one for the new agents—if and when?"

"Precisely."

"Any progress on finding anybody to train there?"

"None that I've heard of lately. The PM promised me a report ten days ago, but nothing's come through."

"Well, with the election coming up the man must have a lot on his mind."

"To be sure." That was one of the reasons J had not only made Richard Blade one of MI6's top agents, but also loved him like a son. Richard could always guess what the other person might be doing, and why. It was a social asset at home and a survival skill in the field. It could help a man charm a hostess at a Mayfair cocktail party and outwit a Russian SMERSH agent in the mountains of Czechoslovakia. Blade had done both.

"In any case," J continued, "I'd like you to meet me for lunch at my club. Say noon tomorrow. Lord Leighton will be there also."

"I'll be there, sir."

"Fine, Richard, fine."

J shut off the radio-telephone, started the car, and wheeled the Rover down the driveway and out through the front gate. The roof of the big sprawling eighteenth century house shone in the sun after the morning's rain. J grinned. The young earl who now ruled that house might scoff at patriotism and "doing his bit for England," but he had just done it in spite of himself. He had given Project Dimension X something it had been seeking for quite some time.

Actually, Project Dimension X had been seeking quite a number of different and sometimes incompatible things for quite a long time. Sometimes the Project reminded J of a gigantic fox-hunt over a mist-shrouded and treacherous field, with only a dozen or so hunters and at least twenty foxes. You couldn't hope to catch all of the beasts, but you could at least try chivying them all along in more or less the same direction.

But there was no doubt that helping Project Dimension X was helping England. In a nutshell, the Project involved sending a man into a succession of alternate dimensions, to survive or die. Hopefully he would survive and explore the dimension. And if it had resources or techniques or devices unknown in home dimension, he would bring them back to England with him.

Dropping down from the abstract to the concrete details (all ten thousand of them or so), Project Dimension X was a little less simple. It had begun by accident the day Lord Leighton connected Richard Blade's mind to a computer. Lord Leighton had been and still was England's most brilliant scientist—not to mention the most maddening one to work with. He had conceived the idea of creating a combination of human and electronic intelligences, superior to either man or computer alone. Well and good.

For the experiment he had needed the most nearly perfect physical and mental specimen he could find. That specimen had been Richard Blade. With nearly twenty years as a top MI6 agent already under his belt, Blade had forgotten more about survival than most men could ever learn. Leighton plugged his specimen into the computer—and Blade wound up in what came to be called Dimension X. He arrived as naked as the day he was born, but his superb mind and body kept him alive. Eventually Lord Leighton was able to reverse the process that had sent Blade winging off into Dimension X. Blade came back to England, back to the computer complex under the Tower of London. It had been very simple, the first time.

But Project Dimension X promptly started shooting out complications in all directions, like the tentacles of an

5

octopus. England's best scientists were unable to duplicate any of the samples of advanced materials or technology that Blade brought home from Dimension X. Sooner or later they would make a breakthrough, of course. But in the meantime the Prime Minister was not particularly happy. He had to justify the millions of pounds the Project had swallowed to inquisitive members of Parliament, so his unhappiness was hardly surprising.

It might have helped if they had been able to send Blade back to the same dimension again and again. But so far that was impossible. They had to fire him off in the general direction of Dimension X and hope he would land somewhere he could survive. This "shooting into the blind" improved neither the efficiency of the Project nor the tempers of Lord Leighton, J, the Prime Minister, or Richard Blade.

And of course there was always the problem of Blade himself. Not that there was anything wrong with him. He had suffered psychological problems of various sorts at one time—drinking, impotence, and the like. That was the result of unexpected reactions of his brain to the computer. But he seemed to have stabilized now. After fourteen successive trips into Dimension X, he was still the most nearly perfect physical and mental specimen available.

And *that* was the problem about Blade. He was too perfect. In fact, he was the only man in the free world who could travel into Dimension X and return alive and sane. Even if J hadn't been concerned for Blade personally, this was a situation that had to be changed. Preferably as fast as possible. If Blade's luck ever ran out in Dimension X, the Project would come to a screeching halt. What the devil, it would come to a halt if Blade were run over by a bloody London taxi!

So a search was on—had been on for two years now—for somebody to take Blade's place. Preferably several "somebodies." Once they had a regular team of Dimension X travelers, Blade could retire. Perhaps he could handle the

6

training end of the Project? Or perhaps if he did go into Dimension X, he could go as the team leader? That was a possibility. Had Leighton done any thinking about any techniques for sending several men through the computer at once? Probably. Leighton tended to think of all sorts of wild hares. And he tended to ask for money to help him chase all of them, too.

But however they were to be used, the new men were badly needed. Sooner or later the combined efforts of J and the Prime Minister would turn them up. And then they would need training. Training of a highly specialized and unorthodox sort. Training which they had not received in their Secret Service or CIA or Special Forces or Royal Marine Commando schools. Nor could they receive it in any of those conventional facilities, without risking compromising Project Dimension X. How do you explain why an agent is being trained in the use of medieval broadsword, longbow, and battleaxe?

So they would need a special training center, one for the Project alone, one where they could learn all the exotic miscellany of skills they would need in Dimension X. J's purchase had just taken care of the land for that. But he would have a good deal more to do before there was a training center out there in Herefordshire. He would need to go over the house and grounds with a fine-tooth comb. Then he would have to confer with Blade, with the best trainers in MI6, with the Project's psychologists. They would all have ideas on what the center would need. He wanted to pick their brains as thoroughly as possible before moving in as much as one stick of furniture.

And perhaps the estate would be good for more than a training center. Every one of Lord Leighton's new ideas meant more paperwork, more office space, more laboratory space. There wasn't much room left in the underground complex below the Tower. What there was, they were reserving for the computer itself. That monster could not be moved at all, at least not without a million-pound bill and a year's delay in the Project. Nor could they expand the complex much farther—at least not without another huge bill. Carving tunnels and chambers out of London's bedrock wasn't cheap.

Moving some of the laboratories and things out to Herefordshire was definitely worth considering. The estate could become a whole annex to the London complex, taking some of the strain off it. Annex West. Yes, that might be a good name. And it certainly was a good idea. It was such a good idea, in fact, that J kept thinking it over all the way back to London.

CHAPTER TWO

"Well, Richard, what do you say to the notion?"

Blade straightened slightly in the Chippendale chair and raised his eyes from his empty plate to J's elegantly wrinkled face.

"I'll be more than willing to help, sir. I think it's a damned good idea, getting a training center set up beforehand. I hope the PM will swallow it."

"He won't have to," put in Lord Leighton, his eyes gleaming wickedly like those of an old billy goat. "We pulled the entire purchase price out of the Contingency Fund. He won't know a thing about it until after the deed is signed, sealed, and delivered."

"To be sure," said J dryly. His eyes met Blade's for a moment. Both knew there was little love lost between Lord Leighton and the Prime Minister. The scientific genius and the hardheaded practical politician had come into head-on collision more than once. "But the bill for fitting the place out as a training center and office annex is going to be more than the Contingency Fund can provide. That's why I want Richard's help. He's our one and only Dimension X veteran. He can sit down with the headshrinkers and the training technicians and give them some notion of what to train the new people for. Otherwise they'll simply be guessing. And we're going to have to give the PM a complete presentation and an accurate one, with a list of gear and a budget.

Otherwise I can't imagine he'll play. He'll say it's another of your wild-goose chases, Leighton."

The scientist ran his gnarled fingers through his fringes of white hair and shook his head. "That's all very well, J. But you can't have Richard now. The computer is all set up with a new program. I was planning to ask him to report tomorrow afternoon."

There was no need for Leighton to say what he wanted Blade to report for. Blade felt a quickening of his breath and for a moment his mouth was so dry that he was not sure he could speak. He was going into Dimension X again—on his fifteenth trip, this time. How many more, he wondered, before one of the people to be trained at this new center replaced him—or his luck ran out? For a moment his vision blurred. The little private dining room, the dark paneling, the white tablecloth, the red wine in the crystal glasses—all seemed to be things from a dream.

Blade took a deep breath, and gradually felt himself return to normal. He didn't like getting the wind up this way, but he was used to it now. He'd be a cast-iron bloody fool if he *liked* being fired off into Dimension X, that was certain. He turned his attention back to the discussion between Leighton and J.

It was a discussion now bordering on an argument. In fact, somebody who didn't know the two men involved would have said they were both working themselves into a foul temper. Blade knew them both too well to believe that. Neither of them would ever give up an argument without stating his position clearly and at length, and neither would push an argument beyond that point. Once each knew where the other stood, they would settle down to hammer out a compromise. Project Dimension X, and what it might do for England, was too important for anything else. So Blade listened, and tried to keep an amused smile off his face as he did so.

"Now damn it, Leighton," J was sayin,"anyone would think you didn't want us to come up with more people besides Richard."

"That's nonsense and you know it perfectly well," retorted

10

the scientist. "It's just that I can't see delaying a mission that's all ready to go so Richard can do a simple consultant's job."

"Why not? Particularly when he's the *only* one who can do this job?"

"If you're going to insist on bringing the Project to a standstill every time you develop some new notion—"

"You're certainly the last person to talk about new notions. What was the bill for your last proposed sub-Project?"

To that Leighton could not come up with a quick reply. He glowered in mock fury at J, then painfully levered himself up out of his chair. On his polio-twisted legs he walked with surprising speed twice around the table. His hunchback was visible under a tweed coat old enough to have been worn at Queen Victoria's funeral. Then he sat back down, fixed J with a penetrating stare from those large and surprisingly alive eyes, and grinned.

"A point well taken, J. Now—how long is this really going to take, with Richard?"

J was about to speak when Blade broke in. "It seems to me there's no need at all to delay the mission. If the estate is as run-down as J says, I imagine it would be wise to get a surveyor and an architect to give it a thorough going-over. Otherwise we might wind up putting in a new office one day and then having the whole thing drop through the floor the next. That would be rather embarrassing. And of course you'll be wanting to set up full security arrangements before you even start surveying. All this will take time. And in the meantime I can head out to Dimension X and be back—"

"In time for tea?" interrupted Leighton with a grin. "Quite so, quite so. Well, J?"

J nodded. "It seems reasonable enough, if it's all right with Richard. And if there's any—delay—in getting you back, we can go ahead with some of the planning anyway."

It was obvious to Blade that J was simply trying to remind Leighton that Blade was not his property, to be sent hither and thither like a case of canned asparagus. Blade appreciated J's efforts, but he couldn't see the point of them.

11

All his debriefings after Dimension X missions were down on tape where any trainer or psychologist could settle down with a beer and play them to his heart's content. And he didn't want to spend days or weeks waiting around for "consultation" with a Dimension X mission hanging over his head. He wanted to go down into the complex, into the computer, and into Dimension X as quickly as possible.

He did just that the next afternoon. The preliminary routine was the same as it had been fourteen times before. In fact, the preliminary routine was threatening to become a crashing bore. But not even Lord Leighton knew that much about Dimension X or the processes that would put Blade there. Not even Lord Leighton could say for certain if leaving out any of the procedures would help or hinder. So Blade and the scientist went through the same old routine with the conscientious care of fighter pilots doing preflight checks on their planes.

Blade goes into the changing booth—check.

Blade strips himself naked—check.

Blade smears foul-smelling black grease all over his body, to prevent electrical burns—check.

Blade leaves the changing booth and sits down in the master chair—check. (And as usual, the chair sitting in its glass booth reminds him of an electric chair, and the rubber of the chair's seat is cold against his bare bottom.)

Lord Leighton comes up to the booth and busies himself attaching cobra-headed electrodes all over Blade's body— check. (And as usual, by the time Leighton finishes, Blade looks as though he is being overgrown by some bizarre tropical growth. Wires of a dozen different colors run off from the electrodes into the guts of the computer.)

Lord Leighton steps back, surveys his work with both care and pride, and then goes over to the master console—check.

Blade leaned back in the chair as far as the attached electrodes would let him, and stared upward. The vast computer consoles in their crackled gray finish loomed over him like the ruins of some abandoned and forgotten city.

Lord Leighton, standing at the main console in his dirty white lab smock, looked like some cheerful gnome inhabiting the ruins. Blade took a deep breath, and forced as much of the tension out of his body as he could. From this point on there was no routine. He could not predict, he could only hope to survive.

Leighton turned toward him. For a moment Blade thought the scientist was going to ask if he was ready. But the questions appeared only in Leighton's eyes, not on his lips. And Blade replied in the same way, nodding silently. Leighton's gnarled hand flexed once or twice, then came down. The red master switch came down with it.

As the switch moved, a low muted whine rose up from somewhere far below. It filled Blade's ears and made his teeth ache. It sounded like a gigantic dentist's drill, and in instinctive reaction Blade shut his eyes and clenched his fists.

But no sharp pain seared through any of his teeth. Instead the whine increased in volume until it was a deafening roar. Now it sounded more like a jet engine winding up for takeoff than any kind of drill. Blade felt the blackness around him become tangible and start to shake and quiver and pulse against his skin. It was like being in an immense bowl of jellied soup that someone was shaking violently. And all the while the whining roar tore at his ears.

The sound rose still further, and Blade knew that his mouth was open and he was screaming in agony as it tore through him. This was sound that could reduce a man's eardrums to powder, his brain to jelly, his whole body to an oozing red paste. If the sound was real, Blade knew he had only a few more seconds to live. But the terrible whine filled his brain so completely that there was no room left in it for any kind of fear or panic.

The sound rose yet further. It passed the point where Blade's brain would accept it any more. Silence fell down on Blade like an enormous weight, crushing him down into blackness.

13

CHAPTER THREE

Blade first became aware of the sound of insects. They were in the long grass that rose up around his aching head, whining softly to themselves. Hearing them was an agreeable surprise. After the nightmare sounds of his transition from home dimension, he would not have been surprised to wind up deaf. Perhaps the sound had never had any physical reality? It might have been merely a hallucination produced by his brain as it writhed in the grip of Lord Leighton's computer.

The grass was not only long, it was stiff and sharp. Blade felt it prickling and jabbing against his bare skin. Slowly, painfully aware of his throbbing head, he sat up and looked around him. The movement startled the insects around him into silence or frantic efforts to escape. Some of them flew across his field of vision, bright darting splotches of red, black, and purple. The whine and hum from the grass died away as he became more aware of his surroundings.

It was just after dawn, with a morning mist hanging low over the ground. A yellow glow higher up told of the rising sun, and patches of blue sky promised a clear day. But in the swirling grayness of the mist, six gigantic dark shapes loomed up tall and grim. They soared up to incredible heights—a mile or more, if Blade was judging their distance correctly in the mist. But even through the mist their outlines were too regular to be natural.

As the mist began to lift, Blade realized that he was standing almost at the base of the seventh of the gigantic towers. The seven formed a huge circle, a good three miles in diameter. In the middle of the circle Blade could make out a sunken, cleared space about half a mile across. The sunken circle seemed as bare, flat, and featureless as a military parade ground. It was paved—with a yellowish coating that reflected more and more brightly the rising sun.

Blade turned his eyes upward, to examine the tower looming over him. He had to crane his neck until it ached, to see the top. In fact, looking up at it gave him a sickening moment of vertigo. It rose so high from such a slender base that Blade almost expected it to stagger suddenly, to topple over on him and crush him into the rocks and vegetation around its base.

All seven seemed to be as identical as seven automobiles of the same make and model turned out on the same assembly line, except for their colors. The one towering above Blade was a glossy dark green that reminded him of a ripe avocado. From left to right around the circle, the other six gleamed orange, dark blue, golden yellow, flaming red, somber flat black, and glossy white. Except for the black one, all seven were so highly polished that the sun blazing off their towering sides struck painfully into Blade's eyes.

Each of the seven rose well over a mile from a base not more than five hundred feet square. Blade did not know very much about architecture, but he could recognize a building technology decades or centuries beyond anything known in home dimension. How had these seven towers come to be where they were, apparently all by themselves? The mist had almost entirely lifted now. He could see no signs of any other buildings beyond the circle of towers, or any signs that the towers themselves were inhabited.

Blade looked up at the green tower above him again. As he did, his doubts about whether these monsters were inhabited were suddenly answered. Around each of the seven towers, two hundred feet or so above the ground, ran a two-story balcony, jutting out some fifty feet or so on all four sides of the towers. Dark figures were appearing on the balcony above Blade, dwarfed by the distance. Blade could not at first even tell whether he was seeing human beings or some more fanciful and perhaps much less agreeable creatures.

Then one of the figures stepped to the edge of the balcony. Without stopping or hesitating, he stepped out into space. Blade suppressed a gasp and watched. He expected to see the figure plunge downward, to smash itself among the rocks and shrubs at the foot of the tower.

Instead, the figure seemed to float slowly, as if it had no more weight than a soap bubble. As it descended, Blade realized that it was in fact human. The man was dressed from head to foot in the same glossy dark green as the finish of his tower. Blade thought he could also see a sword blade on the man's belt, flashing in the sun.

For a moment he wondered if he should take cover and wait to see what happened. Certainly there was room to hide around the base of the tower. A belt of tumbled boulders, shrubs and small trees, long grass, and little gullies and hills extended for nearly a mile around the base of the green tower. The other six also seemed to be surrounded by such a fringe of semi-wilderness. Did these people preserve those tracts for recreational purposes—as parks—or was it that they simply didn't care? Blade remembered the Sleepers of the Dimension of Dreams, and how they had let an entire city crumble to ruins while they sank into their Dreams.

Blade decided that he was trying to analyze not only ahead of the facts, but at the wrong time. The man in green was less than a hundred feet above Blade's head now, and descending steadily. He was definitely wearing a sword—no, two swords—at his belt. On his head was a cylindrical helmet with cheek pieces and a crest from which a green plume waved. A warrior, obviously.

Now Blade understood how the man was descending so effortlessly through the air. He was riding down on a kind of flying trapeze. Three stout bars of glossy green metal formed an equilateral triangle. The warrior stood on one of these and clung to straps fastened to the two side-pieces. Blade could see no rope or wire attached to the trapeze. Had these people conquered gravity, like the alien Menel in the world of the Ice Dragons? That was an intriguing thought, but Blade reminded himself sharply that this was not the time for analysis or speculation.

Should he duck for cover or go forward to meet the warrior? It was almost too late to hide. Besides, he had to make his first encounter with the inhabitants of this Dimension sooner or later. The odds were good on their having something worth taking back to home dimension. Advanced civilizations usually did, and these people seemed to be quite highly advanced.

As Blade reached this decision, the warrior in green reached the ground. He did not ride his trapeze down the last few feet, but instead jumped while it was still eight feet above the ground. He landed and rolled like a trained tumbler or paratrooper. Blade mentally noted this as suggesting a high level of training among this Dimension's warriors. The man was up again almost instantly, and as the trapeze settled to the ground beside him, he snatched it up and held the upper end of the triangle against his face. There was apparently a microphone in the trapeze, but the warrior's voice boomed out loud enough to have been heard on the balcony two hundred feet above without any electronic help. Certainly Blade heard it clearly enough, as he crouched behind a bush a good one hundred feet away.

"I, Kir-Noz, Warrior of the First Rank of the Tower of the Serpent, declare that I am First on the Ground this day of war against the Tower of the Eagle. Let those who have the keeping of the Book of Honor record this day." The warrior dropped the trapeze and spread his arms wide, drawing his two swords as he did so. They flashed in the sun, a long sword and a shorter one, both curved, both with green-enameled hilts. Then he thrust the swords back in their scabbards and began to walk slowly away from the base of the tower, his eyes on the ground.

He had covered perhaps fifty feet when Blade rose from

17

behind his concealing bush. The warrior's eyes opened in amazement, staring at this unexpected apparition. His jaw sagged so that his mouth gaped open like that of an idiot or a dying fish. Blade took two steps forward and held out both hands, palms outward in a gesture of peace.

"Greetings, warrior," said Blade. He could be certain that the warrior would understand his language as well as he understood the warrior's. During the transition into Dimension X the parts of Blade's brain that controlled his language skills changed. As a result of these changes, Blade reached each new dimension with an instinctive command of the local language. It no longer surprised him as it had the first few times, although he didn't fully understand the reasons. (Neither did Lord Leighton, in fact.) But it was no less welcome now for the fifteenth time than it had been the first. Sign language was more useful in adventure novels than in survival situations where your life might depend on getting your message across fast and accurately.

Seeing that the warrior was too astonished to reply for the moment, Blade continued. "My name is Blade. I come in peace to the people of the Tower of the Serpent, from a distant land called England. I would speak with the rulers of the Tower of the Serpent."

These words seemed to push the warrior beyond simply standing and goggling at Blade. His jaw closed with a snap and his hands dropped to his sword hilts and closed around them. "You are not of Melnon?"

"What is Melnon?" asked Blade.

The warrior looked as though Blade had just asked, "What is the sun?" or, "What is rain?"

"Melnon is the world," he said sharply. "Are you of the world or are you not?"

"I have come to the world that is Melnon, from England. I have come in peace."

"You say that you come from the Beyond?" The warrior gestured with one hand, outward beyond the circle of towers.

"If all outside the towers of Melnon is the Beyond, then

yes, I do come from the Beyond." Blade wasn't sure whether being from the "Beyond" would get him treated as a monster or as a god. So he was careful to qualify his statements.

Apparently such subtleties were useless, with this warrior at least. "You cannot be from the Beyond. For it is not of the world, and there are no people except in the world. You are of the Low People of one of the other towers. Or perhaps"— the warrior hesitated as if he were about to use obscene language—"one of the other towers has foresworn the War Wisdom of Melnon. They are sending men among the Waste Land at the foot of the Tower of the Serpent, to catch and kill the First on the Ground." Kir-Noz drew both swords and flourished them so that they whistled in the air. "The tower that forgot the War Wisdom of Melnon will pay in time. But you shall pay at once!" Without any further words the man sprang toward Blade.

Blade was not caught by surprise. The moment the swords flashed clear, he had stepped back two paces and dropped into a fighting stance. While Kir-Noz was hurling his threat, Blade was surveying the ground around his own feet, looking for any handy-sized loose stones. There didn't seem to be any. So as Kir-Noz charged him, Blade's leg muscles knotted, and he sailed five feet to the right in a single leap. Kir-Noz was moving too fast to stop. He charged straight through the spot where Blade had been standing. His swords carved the empty air with a fury that would have been frightening if it hadn't been so useless. He pulled himself to a stop, turned, and saw Blade standing off to one side.

Kir-Noz charged again. Blade leaped aside again. Kir-Noz kept on going again. By the time they had gone through the sequence a third time, Blade was beginning to wonder what kind of warrior he was dealing with. He wasn't sure whether Kir-Noz was feeble-minded, half-blind, or simply so badly trained that he had never learned to keep an eye on his opponent. Blade's opinion of the competence of the warriors in this Dimension took a sharp downturn.

Kir-Noz's ineptness would be helpful to Blade. He

19

definitely did not want to kill the warrior. But if Kir-Noz had been at all competent, it would have been difficult for an unarmed man to get inside those two sharp and fast-moving swords. As it was, Blade had plenty of time to consider various tricks. In the meantime, he kept leaping aside from Kir-Noz's bull-like rushes. Many years of unarmed combat training had polished his reflexes and left his leg muscles like steel springs, so he had no worries about being able to go on avoiding Kir-Noz. But he didn't want to simply go on avoiding the warrior, any more than he wanted to kill him.

Little by little, Blade led Kir-Noz through the grass, over the rocks, away from the base of the Tower of the Serpent. He wanted the other men on the balcony high above to see what happened to their picked warrior. When Kir-Noz charged for the ninth time they were a good one hundred yards out from the base, in a small field littered with numerous clods of earth and grass. As Blade sprang aside he dropped into a crouch. His hands darted down and snatched up two clods of dirt. He leaped to his feet again and watched as Kir-Noz pulled himself to a stop once more, then he stood and faced the warrior.

"Ho, Kir-Noz," he shouted. "Here I am, wise warrior of the Tower of the Serpent. Why am I so hard to find?"

The taunt stunned Kir-Noz into an explosion of rage. "When I have killed you, Blade, I will have Queen Mir-Kasa send a message to your home tower. They have done a great wrongness against the War Wisdom of Melnon, to send to watch us a man who carries no swords but only leaps about and waves his arms like a little child of the Low People playing in the dirt!"

"Oh, to be sure," said Blade sarcastically. "My masters no doubt understand nothing of the War Wisdom of Melnon. And when you have killed me you can say anything you want to them. But first you have to kill me. Come on, Kir-Noz! Show me what a warrior of the Tower of the Serpent is good for, besides waving his swords about as though he were chasing flies away from a garbage heap."

That last taunt drove Kir-Noz beyond the limits of speech. He screamed wordlessly, like a wild animal on the hunt, then dashed at Blade. As Kir-Noz charged, Blade's arms snapped up, and the two clods of earth he had been carrying sailed through the air at Kir-Noz's face.

They never reached their target, though. Kir-Noz's eyes flicked toward them as they came at him. Then, between one breath and the next, both his swords whistled up and struck with blinding speed in two crisscrossing slashes. The two clods disintegrated into a spray of dust and chopped bits of grass.

Kir-Noz's speed with his swords had been far faster than Blade had expected. But Blade's own training was better and his reflexes just as lightning-swift. Before the dust from the clods had started hitting the ground, Blade was lunging at Kir-Noz. Pivoting on his left leg, he shot his right leg out at a speed that even Kir-Noz could not match or guard against. Blade's leg outreached the warrior's sword. His foot crashed into Kir-Noz's stomach as the swords arced down. The warrior folded up like a pocketknife and reeled backward several steps, but he held on to his weapons. Blade closed, chopped Kir-Noz across the left wrist to break his grip on the short sword, and snatched it up as it fell.

The sight of one of his swords in Blade's hands seemed to revive Kir-Noz, oddly enough. His breath came more normally, and he straightened up and stared at Blade. Blade returned the stare, with considerable respect. Kir-Noz's training might have its limitations, but he was certainly fast, and he could certainly take punishment.

"Ho, Kir-Noz," Blade said. "Will it violate the War Wisdom of Melnon if I come against you with this sword against the one I have left to you?"

Kir-Noz looked dubious. "It were better for me to consult the Council of Wisdom," he said slowly. "They—"

"Are not here," Blade interrupted him quietly. "Come, Kir-Noz. You call yourself a warrior of the First Rank. Surely that should make you fit and able to decide how to kill an enemy." His voice took on a mocking tone again. "What are the warriors of the First Rank in the Tower of the Serpent? Little children tugging at their mothers' skirts? Perhaps even little children of the Low People?"

Kir-Noz screamed like a maniac, and launched himself at Blade. If he hadn't still been slowed by Blade's kick, Blade might have died in that next instant. As it was, Kir-Noz's long sword whistled down past his ear only inches away. It took a frantic parry with the short sword to keep the return stroke away from his groin. Blade decided to open the distance again.

But now that he had Blade at close quarters, Kir-Noz was the last man in Melnon to let him get clear. He came in again, his sword flashing in a dazzling series of strokes that took all of Blade's strength and skill to parry. Blade found his breath beginning to come more quickly, and his legs protested. As the sun rose higher, sweat began to pour down off him, stinging his eyes and making his hand so slick he began to find it hard to keep a grip on his sword.

He was also becoming aware of two things about his opponent, as the deadly exchange went on. Kir-Noz was wearing completely flexible but obviously tough body armor—glossy green, of course—that covered him from neck to groin. Several times thrusts which should have gone deep into his flesh merely dimpled the armor. And there were few enough chances for those thrusts. In theory a man with a short sword could close in, under the reach of a man with a longer weapon. But if the man with the long sword was as fast as Kir-Noz obviously was, matters weren't so easy. Blade hoped that Kir-Noz would lose some of that speed before long, but nothing of the kind happened. In spite of the punishment he had taken, the Tower warrior seemed to have recovered every bit of his speed and strength. And it began to seem to Blade that Kir-Noz's endurance might just possibly be greater than his own. That was an unpleasant thought. It meant he would have to make his own move before he became more tired and lost too much of his speed.

More important, he wanted to make the move with his sword. It was obvious by now that fighting in Melnon was highly stylized, according to the "War Wisdom." If he wanted to ensure his own reputation and good reception here, he would have to beat Kir-Noz with Melnon's weapons. And he still didn't want to kill the man. He was strong and fast and deadly and, if he were defeated in such a way that he could respect Blade, he would make a valuable ally.

By the time he had worked this all out, Blade knew that he would have to make his move very soon indeed. Twice the tip of Kir-Noz's sword had nicked his flesh, leaving thin, gently oozing gashes. Its edge must be razor-sharp. With the heavy blade behind it, the edge would sheer through flesh and bone as though it were cutting paper. Blade realized that he could hardly risk even the lightest wound from Kir-Noz's sword.

Kir-Noz was wearing calf-length green boots, with heavy soles. And Blade began to notice that Kir-Noz always looked quickly at the ground underfoot before closing. Of course! The man was used to doing all his fighting on level ground. Perhaps that table-flat drill field in the center of the circle was a fighting arena for the warriors of all seven Towers of Melnon? Blade, on the other hand, was barefoot. And he was as agile as a mountain goat at any time, in any place. Step by step, he began to back toward a patch of gravel and small boulders, leading Kir-Noz after him. He ignored the warrior's taunts about "cowards who can fight only against the War Wisdom," and kept on backing. Kir-Noz was by now too intent on finishing this infuriating opponent to be fully aware of where he was going. He kept following Blade as though he were on a leash.

Blade stepped back into the patch of rough ground. He saw Kir-Noz look at the gravel and stones. The warrior recognized the treacherous footing—but he kept coming. He advanced furiously, obviously determined not to waste any more time. He closed so fast that Blade could hardly back away quickly enough.

Then Kir-Noz's left foot came down on an insecure rock. He did not quite stagger, but for a moment it was all he could do to keep on his feet. As his foot slipped off the rock he stepped into a soft patch, sinking so deeply that the gravel was almost halfway up his boot. He lurched to one side, trying desperately to jerk his foot out of the soft spot. As he lurched he was off balance for a moment.

In that moment Blade closed. He lunged at Kir-Noz with the short sword, stabbing straight at the warrior's armored belly with all the speed and strength left in his own body. Simultaneously he chopped with the edge of a flattened hand at Kir-Noz's right arm, the one holding the long sword. Both blows connected. The jolt in his belly toppled Kir-Noz off balance. He went down on his back in the gravel. He lashed upward with his sword, but Blade's down-chopping hand smashed into his sword arm again. Blade felt the bone crack under the blow and heard Kir-Noz gasp as he bit back a scream. Then Blade dropped on his knees beside the fallen warrior and twisted the long sword out of Kir-Noz's hand. Finally he raised the sword and held the point an inch from Kir-Noz's face.

"Well, Kir-Noz. I have fought with your weapons. In fact, I have fought you with a short sword against a long one. What does your War Wisdom say to that?"

Kir-Noz was silent for a moment, biting his lip from the pain of his broken arm. Sweat was pouring off him. Blade undid the straps of the warrior's heavy cylindrical helmet and took it off. That seemed to revive Kir-Noz somewhat.

"I do not know what the War Wisdom says to what you have done, Blade. Perhaps that is because no one in all of Melnon would believe that what you have just done could be done at all. I have been a warrior of the First Rank of the Tower of the Serpent for ten years, in more than fifty wars fought according to the War Wisdom, without ever seeing a warrior such as you. Do you truly claim to be from the Beyond?"

"England is nowhere here in Melnon, that is certain," said Blade with a grin.

Kir-Noz managed a feeble smile in return. "No, it is not. Perhaps you had best say that you are indeed from the Beyond. Otherwise you could only be a warrior of one of the other towers. Perhaps they might even think you one of the Low People fleeing from your station in another tower. And in either case they would kill you. But if you say that you are something which has no place in our law and custom... Well, at least they will not kill you before the Council of Wisdom makes laws to cover such cases as yours. And perhaps they will not kill you at all. Perhaps they—"

Kir-Noz never finished the sentence. In that moment Blade sprang to his feet, both swords flashing. He swore. Kir-Noz painfully raised himself on one elbow and looked around him.

As though they had sprung from the grass and rocks under their feet, some forty green-clad warriors were standing in a wide circle around Blade and Kir-Noz. The expressions on the faces under the helmets were not at all friendly.

CHAPTER FOUR

Blade knew one sick moment of absolute certainty that he was not going to get out of this one. Considering how much trouble disposing of one of them had been, he certainly could not hope to survive an encounter with forty warriors of the Tower of the Serpent. Not even if very few of them were as good as Kir-Noz. Blade knew he was half exhausted, and he was obviously completely surrounded.

How had they managed to get down around him without his seeing them? No doubt there were trapezes all around the Tower's balcony. They could easily have come down on the far side and then come around the Tower on foot. And he had been so preoccupied with Kir-Noz that a herd of elephants might have tramped up to him without attracting his attention.

Blade was just opening his mouth to shout a challenge to the circle of warriors when Kir-Noz raised his own voice in a sharp hail.

"Ho, warriors of the Tower of the Serpent! I, Kir-Noz, warrior of the First Rank, ask what you mean to do with this man!"

The sudden angry question from one of their own people seemed to stun all the warriors in the circle. It was several moments before anyone replied. Then a warrior nearly as tall as Blade himself stepped forward and shouted out his answer.

26

"We shall slay him, Kir-Noz, according to the War Wisdom, and we shall be enrolled in the Book of Honor for doing so. Those who go against the War Wisdom of Melnon must be punished, lest Melnon become weak. And if the Towers of Melnon become weak, the Beyond may break in and make an end of us."

Kir-Noz laughed. "Nris-Pol, I know all that. Remember that I was a warrior of the First Rank when you were still a candidate. Stop reciting the First Lesson in the Book of the War Wisdom to me." Kir-Noz laughed again. "It is too late to defend our tower against the Beyond, for this warrior who defeated me is from the Beyond."

If Kir-Noz had given all forty of the watching warriors an electric shock they could hardly have been more startled. Gasps and murmurs of astonishment and what sounded like oaths rose from all around the circle. The tall warrior named Nris-Pol grimaced. "That is a poor jest, Kir-Noz. There is no human life in the Beyond. If this—thing—is a being indeed from the Beyond, then we shall not treat it as a warrior according to the War Wisdom. We shall call in a master to administer it, as if it were one of the Low People." He turned to one of his men. "Go, use the far-speaker, and call the First Master." The man was turning to leave, when Kir-Noz raised his voice to a roar.

"Hold, you fools! I was First on the Ground today, and I have been a warrior of the First Rank longer than any I see here. Certainly longer than that wind-filled bag Nris-Pol! You shall stay and hear me, and you shall not depart without my leave or I will speak to the Council of Wisdom about you. And indeed the War Wisdom is sacred, and the council's way with those who violate it is short, as you will discover if you do not hold your tongue!"

There was more strength in Kir-Noz's voice than Blade had thought could be left in his whole body. The warriors of the circle stopped dead at his words—even Nris-Pol. In the silence Kir-Noz went on. "This man is not a warrior of another tower sent to our Waste Land in violation of the

War Wisdom, for he has skills in war that no warrior of the Towers of Melnon has ever had in our fifteen generations."

"All the more reason to kill him, then," shouted Nris-Pol. "He will corrupt us, lead the candidates astray, into paths contrary to the War Wisdom."

"Do not be so sure of that, Nris-Pol," snapped Kir-Noz. "Consider how after he drove me back the first time, he took up a proper sword and beat me with it. One sword, and a short one at that, against my long sword. He defeated me with that, me, Kir-Noz, one hundred and seventeen times victor in the wars."

"And victor over you, Nris-Pol, in a dozen practice bouts," someone called out. "When was the last time you beat *him,* Nris-Pol?" Nris-Pol growled savagely in reply.

Kir-Noz continued. "And then when he had me flat on my back on the ground, he had speech with me, instead of killing me slowly. That means he cannot be one of the Low People who by some chance has learned a warrior's arts. Even one of the Low People of the Tower of the Leopard would never have spared a warrior of another tower. And the Low People of any other tower would have gelded me with a dull knife and plucked out my eyes with their thumbs before slaying me. You know this well, all of you. You have seen what the Low People in their wrath can do."

"In their rebellion against the Peace Wisdom," snapped Nris-Pol. "And it proves nothing that this—thing—did not slay you. He would have known that he was in full sight of the warriors of the Tower of the Serpent, and what we would do to him if he slew you. There was no mercy in him, only fear."

"Nonsense," snapped Kir-Noz. "Were he one of the Low People, no fear of anything we might do to him would have held him back. His life was already forfeit for escape and for raising his hand against me. What more did he have to lose? You well know how a man with nothing to lose is made desperate and all the more dangerous."

"Beware, Kir-Noz," roared Nris-Pol. "You speak too

softly of the Low People. Remember what happened to your brother Bryg-Noz before you go on in this fashion."

"Bryg-Noz was as loyal a keeper of the War and Peace Wisdoms alike as could be found in all of Melnon," Kir-Noz replied sharply. "You know that well. And you know why he was sent among the Low People. You coveted his position in Queen Mir-Kasa's bed. But I have heard that though you have his position now, you have not his *positions*. And Her Splendor is not pleased with that—or with you. Perhaps she will soon find an excuse to send you down among the Low People."

That string of insults reduced Nris-Pol to incoherent shriekings and stammerings. The other warriors looked on. And Blade could see amusement on the faces of many of them. Kir-Noz's tongue seemed to be as sharp and fast-moving as his swords. As Nris-Pol spluttered away into silence a heavy-set, barrel-chested warrior with gray hair showing under his helmet spoke up.

"All that you say may be wise, Kir-Noz, but do we have time for dealing with the matter at such length now? It lacks but little of the fourth hour, and at the fourth hour we are to meet the warriors of the Tower of the Eagle in the Plain of War. If we spend much more time here talking, we shall not have time to choose a warrior to replace you. Then we must either go forth to have our war with the Eagles with one man less than they, or give up five man-points from the outset for being late. Unless you think you can still fight?"

Kir-Noz shook his head. "My right arm is broken, Pen-Jerg."

Pen-Jerg shrugged. "Then let us send this man who has defeated you upward and have him kept among the Low People until the day's war is over. We can deal with him more properly at some later time."

Again Kir-Noz shook his head, this time angrily. "That would be to dishonor and disgrace a man who is certainly a mighty warrior. Shame would take him, take his war skills from him, were we to send him among the Low People."

"That is true," said Pen-Jerg. "But is there any other way?"

"Yes," said Kir-Noz. "I cannot fight today against the Eagles. Let this man fight them in my place. Perhaps he does not understand every word of the War Wisdom. But you all saw him fighting, I think. Would you not say that he has the War Wisdom in his soul?"

Pen-Jerg nodded, and he was not the only one. But Nris-Pol let out another animal growl and shouted, "You are fools to listen to this nonsense! The Eagles—"

"So I speak nonsense, and your fellow chosen warriors of this day are fools? Well, well, Nris-Pol. Would you care to go before the Council of Wisdom and say the same words again?" That shut Nris-Pol up as efficiently as hitting him over the head could have done. Blade could see relief on the faces of most of the warriors in the circle. They had obviously been getting tired of Nris-Pol's snappings and snarlings and bad temper.

Kir-Noz went on briskly. "As Pen-Jerg says, the Eagles will not wait forever. It is in the War Wisdom that if all the warriors of a day's war party choose a new man, he may be exempted from the formal rites. Will you all give your voices for this man?"

"I certainly will," said Pen-Jerg. "And I urge all of you to do likewise. We all know Kir-Noz to be a man of honor and much knowledge of the War and Peace Wisdoms both. I will not set my judgment up against his in the matter of this man. I choose him to join us, to make up the number of our war party for this day's war with the Eagles."

"I choose him also," said a warrior standing next to Pen-Jerg.

"And I!"

"And I also."

"I do choose him."

The cries of assent went rapidly around the circle, until it came to be Nris-Pol's turn. Kir-Noz motioned to Blade to bend down, and whispered in his ear. "If he says 'No,' then that is an end to it. I can say nothing for you, since the War

30

Wisdom says the choice must be altogether free." Blade nodded, but he could not help wondering whether this mass of rules and customs called the War Wisdom really deserved the name. "War Folly" might be more accurate. And if the "Peace Wisdom" that governed the civil affairs of Melnon was as complex and convoluted, God knows what things must be like inside the towers!

While Blade was considering this, Nris-Pol was considering his vote: It was obvious that the decision was costing him a good deal of effort. Finally he shrugged his shoulders and growled, "Very well. The chaos from Beyond may break into Melnon for this day's work. But I will not stand apart from your folly—for now. I choose this man."

That ended any danger of opposition. Within a few more minutes the whole party had chosen Blade. He stood up and stared around ·him at the circle of men who had suddenly become his comrades, according to a set of strange customs he still hardly understood.

"You have done me great honor, to choose me, a man from the Beyond, to join you for this day's war. May any punishment for this choice be visited upon me alone. And may terrible punishment indeed fall upon me if I go against the War Wisdom of the Towers of Melnon."

"It will," growled Nris-Pol. "Don't worry about that."

"Enough," said Kir-Noz. "Blade, you are chosen in my place in the war party. Pen-Jerg, as I cannot go with you this day, I will ask you to wear the commander's plume. You are the most worthy among this company." He reached over to the helmet that Blade had taken from his head and plucked the green plume from its crest. He raised it in his left hand, and Pen-Jerg took it reverently.

Then Kir-Noz unbuckled his belt, and raised it toward Blade. "Blade, you will need both weapons and a belt to carry them in this day's war. As I cannot use mine for the moment, I see no reason why you should not have them. Use them well."

"I am honored," said Blade. He managed a brief bow.

31

"I wish there were time to fit you with proper armor," said Kir-Noz. "You are in terrible danger going forth with nothing but a belt and two swords."

"I doubt that," said Blade. "Unless there is a warrior among the Eagles as good as you are, I expect to be back without a scratch on me." That was more confidence than he felt, in truth. But the occasion seemed to call for the pose.

Kir-Noz grinned. "I am not sure that you may not be right. And in any case, the Eagles will get a surprise today. When you come out thus, they will expect you to be easy meat. I wonder how long it will take them to find out otherwise."

"After my first opponent hits the ground," said Blade.

"Well and good, Blade," said Kir-Noz. "Now, Pen-Jerg, have the reel-master send down a lifter, and lead our warriors forth to beat the Eagles." Pen-Jerg bowed his head, then straightened and turned to the other warriors.

"All right, it's time to stop gaping. We've got a war to fight today. Form line and follow me."

CHAPTER FIVE

Blade found his opinion of the tower warriors' training growing unfavorable again as Pen-Jerg led them away from the base of the tower and through the Waste Land, toward the Plain of War. They made no effort to keep any sort of orderly formation, but marched in a long, straggling single line. Forty warriors trailed out over a space of more than a hundred yards like a class of schoolchildren on an outing. In fact, it was almost too charitable to describe the warriors' progress as a march. They made no effort to set or keep a cadence, and in their heavy boots they stumbled and lurched drunkenly over rough ground that the barefooted Blade crossed easily.

Blade could not help wondering what would happen to this ragged collection of individually skilled fighting men if they were ambushed on the way through the Waste Land. Of course in daylight the men on the balcony could see anything that moved on the ground near the base of the tower. But suppose one of the other towers sent over fifty men by night, and concealed them in the bushes and gullies near the outer edge of the Waste Land? There was enough room to hide a battalion there, and plenty of places for a surprise attack. He mentioned this possibility to Pen-Jerg.

The Serpent warrior's jaw dropped and a gasp of pure horror came out of his open mouth. "Don't ever say such things aloud, warrior—ah, what did Kir-Noz call you?"

"Blade. Of England."

"Blade, then. It would be impossible for the other towers to think of something so monstrous. They—they would be hurling defiance to the War Wisdom."

Blade nodded. He decided against going on to suggest that if the other towers couldn't use ambush tactics, the Tower of the Serpent should take advantage of the fact. Ambush tactics were contrary to the War Wisdom, and that was that. This explained, of course, why the area around the towers was so wild and overgrown. It didn't matter to any of the tower warriors, because they knew that none of their opponents would ever take advantage of natural cover. And—

"Are all your wars fought on the Plain of War?"

Pen-Jerg gave Blade the kind of look one gives a child or an idiot who has just tried to ask a question. "Of course. Is it otherwise where—" his voice dropped to a half-whisper "—you come from?" Apparently Pen-Jerg would not commit himself to believing the strange tales of Blade's origins.

"Certainly. We fight wherever each side thinks it can do so to the greatest advantage."

"What happens if the two sides seek different places?"

"Then sometimes there is no war at all. On the other hand, sometimes one side gets to its chosen place before the other one does. Then it can sometimes win a very great victory, at a small cost."

"That hardly seems fair," said Pen-Jerg. His tone was that of a man who hears another talking folly, but is trying to be polite about it.

"I know," said Blade. "But war among the English is not fought to be fair, or in keeping with some War Wisdom. When we fight, we fight to win, and all our people go to the war."

Once again Pen-Jerg was unable to keep an expression of horror off his face. "Your Low People, too?"

"What *are* Low People?"

"Those without honor or wisdom, Blade. Those unfit to go to war. Those fit only to clean the halls and levels of the towers and to serve the High People, who possess honor and wisdom. Do you—are you trying to tell me that in England—there are no Low People?" Pen-Jerg's voice was that of a man trying to conceive of the inconceivable.

"That is almost true," said Blade.

Pen-Jerg threw up his hands—literally. Obviously he wasn't sure whether he was dealing with a fool, a madman, or an extremely cunning man whose people's customs he could never in a century hope to understand. And it obviously didn't matter much to him. He strode along in silence for a time, then turned back to Blade.

"Look you, Blade," he said in a low voice. "Perhaps you are telling the truth. Perhaps you are telling lies. I don't care. But I will ask you, by the War and Peace Wisdom alike, to say no more of what war or peace are like in England—or wherever you come from. Few among our people would understand you. And half of those who did would haul you before the Council of Wisdom and Queen Mir-Kasa for judgment. Then you could expect to be sent down among the Low People. After that you would be degraded forever and you could never be a warrior again. And I would grieve to see the Tower of the Serpent lose such a warrior as you seem to be simply because you cannot keep your tongue still."

"But—" began Blade.

"Enough," said Pen-Jerg. "Remember what was said of a warrior called Bryg-Noz?"

"I did not know that he was a warrior."

"He was. The greatest of the past ten-year, by far, greater even than his brother Kir-Noz, who is the greatest among us now. He was Kir-Noz's elder brother, Principal Chooser, Guide to the Candidates, Steward to Queen Mir-Kasa. There seemed to be nothing in the Tower of the Serpent beyond his reach and grasp. But he fell. He fell because, like you, he would not give over questioning the War Wisdom by which we fight our war, or the Peace Wisdom by which each

Tower of Melnon is divided into the High People and the Low People. Except for the Tower of the Leopard," Pen-Jerg added, with distaste in his voice.

"I see," said Blade. He actually did not see much more than the wisdom of following Pen-Jerg's advice and keeping his mouth shut. But for the moment that was enough.

"Good," said Pen-Jerg. "Keep silent, and though you may be from—some place—you may yet become a warrior of the Towers of Melnon." He turned back to the line of warriors. "In the name of the Wisdoms, hurry! We're not going to lose man-points simply by letting those cursed Eagles reach the Plain ahead of us."

The warriors behind them broke into a run, clumping and lumbering along in their heavy boots, sometimes stumbling and sprawling on the ground. Blade's mind could not help returning to the image of the ambush. If a force of tower warriors was ever attacked in the Waste Lands, half of them would break their necks falling over their own feet before a single sword touched them!

The warriors of the Tower of the Serpent rushed across the last few hundred yards of their tower's Waste Land and reached the edge of the Plain of War. Pen-Jerg called a halt there, and stared out toward the center of the Plain.

From the edge of the Waste Land the ground sloped sharply down to the level of the Plain nearly a hundred feet below. The slope was all grass, thick and as neatly-trimmed as a suburban lawn, in vivid contrast to the yellow coating of the Plain. The grass strip was nearly a hundred yards wide and divided into seven sections by lines of pink stones. Yes, definitely pink. The color at first seemed ridiculous to Blade. Then he realized that against the green it was probably the most visible color not already associated with one of the seven towers.

Five of the sections were already dotted with moving colored specks—people, no doubt, dressed in the colors of their tower. The Serpents' section and the one directly across from it were both empty. Blade noticed that pale green

36

flowers had been planted in the Serpents' section in the form of a gigantic snake with its head raised to strike. In the Eagles' section, on the other hand, was the enormous white silhouette of an eagle. Then as he looked, he saw a line of white specks moving down into the Eagles' section. The opposition in the day's war had arrived. Pen-Jerg raised his hand, and motioned the line of Serpents forward down the slope.

As they scrambled down to the Plain, Blade could not help asking Pen-Jerg one more question.

"Why are the sections of the Serpents and Eagles empty, Pen-Jerg?"

Pen-Jerg apparently recognized this question as coming from legitimate curiosity. "The War Wisdom has it thus, Blade. For it is the great fear that if the people of the towers actually fighting the war were to come to see it, they might become angry when they saw their tower losing. They might run on to the Plain and join the fight, and make the war an uncontrollable slaughter, like the wars you say you have in England."

"Particularly the Low People, I suppose."

"What are you thinking of, Blade?" said Pen-Jerg sharply. "You must realize that the Low People never leave their towers. They are not taught to use the lifters or the reels. The Peace Wisdom forbids it. They could only leap from the balconies and die among the stones of the Waste Land below. No, it is the anger of the High People that the War Wisdom guards us against. To fight under the eyes of warriors only from the other towers keeps those actually in the war from violating the War Wisdom."

"I can see that," said Blade. "But what if the warriors of one of the other towers favor the victory of one of the warring towers more than the other?"

"That also is against the War Wisdom," said Pen-Jerg. "That is called an 'Alliance,' and any tower urging it would find itself rejected at once. In fact, it would find itself dishonored, and any of its warriors captured in war would be sent down among the Low People of those who captured them. But enough questions, Blade. We are almost into the War Circle."

Blade nodded and fell silent. Most of the things he felt like saying were in any case better left unsaid. Obedience to the War Wisdom must be rather precarious, considering how unnatural most of it seemed. That the War Wisdom had endured as basic law among the towers for fifteen generations was a miracle. But perhaps they could be—

Blade shut off that thought. This was the wrong time and place for it. Besides, if the people of the towers were happy with this apparently preposterous system—well, that was their problem. He was not going to try to play games with it, at least not before he knew a great deal more. And in the meantime there was a war to fight—and to live through.

The actual Plain was divided into seven segments by more lines of pink stones. Still more stones outlined a circle about three hundred yards in diameter in the very center of the Plain. As the Serpent warriors jogged toward the circle, Blade saw that its surface was scuffed as if scarred by many booted feet. He suddenly realized that he was within minutes of entering a fight whose rules he didn't know.

"Pen-Jerg," he said quickly. "Is there any part of the War Wisdom in particular that I must know to fight in this war?"

"The fighting is the simplest part of the War Wisdom," said Pen-Jerg. "If the Eagles accept that you were properly chosen and can use Kir-Noz's weapons, you will have no real problems."

"Yes," said Blade patiently. "I can see that. But how is the war actually fought?"

Again Blade got a look as though he had been a half-wit. "The only way it is lawful to fight a war. Each Tower lines its warriors up in four lines of ten men apiece. The man at the head of each line fights his opponent until one or the other falls. Then the second man in each line fights likewise, and so on. You must use the two swords, and you must not try to get around to your opponent's back."

"I see," said Blade. "And how long does this—go on?" He very nearly said "this nonsense."

"Until all the men on one side have fought, or until one side has won so many fights that the other could not hope to catch up."

"And the side which yields or runs out of men first loses the war?"

"You understand it exactly. Are you sure the English have never fought like this?"

"Not exactly." The only people he knew of who had tried to fight this way in real battles were the medieval French knights. And the English longbow had punctured their pretensions, their tactics, and the knights themselves all very thoroughly. He wondered how long it would be before something equally drastic happened to this stylized, rule-bound game the people of the towers called "war."

Now the warriors of both sides were approaching the center of the marked-off circle. The warriors of the Tower of the Eagle were dressed identically to those of the Tower of the Serpent, down to the last detail. But everything they wore was glossy white, and their commander wore a long white plume in the crest of his helmet.

Two seconds later the commander apparently caught sight of Blade. He shouted "Halt!" and his entire column stopped dead and piled up behind him. Their eyes switched back and forth between Blade and their own commander as he stepped out in front of them and hailed Pen-Jerg.

"What is this—whatever or whoever he is—you are bringing practically naked to a war, Pen-Jerg? And why do you wear the commander's plume anyway? I thought Kir-Noz was to command the Serpents today?"

"He was, Commander Zef-Dron. But he chose to be First on the Ground also. In the Waste Lands he met this warrior, Blade." Pen-Jerg briefly summarized what had happened. As he mentioned Blade's being chosen to fill Kir-Noz's place, the other commander shook his head wearily.

"When you said this naked—man—had defeated Kir-

Noz, I thought you were trying to make a bad joke worse. But you have said that he was chosen, and even given Kir-Noz's weapons. Do you swear this is true, by the War Wisdom?"

"I do so swear."

Zef-Dron shrugged. "Then I cannot by the War Wisdom go against your warrior's choice. Is he planning to fight as he is—naked but for the weapons?"

Blade nodded. "I am."

"I think I will not waste time asking where you get the idea you can do this and survive. Your first opponent will slice you into small pieces. But if you and Pen-Jerg wish your life thrown away..." Zef-Dron shrugged again.

Blade grinned. "Do not count your victories—or your surviving men—Zef-Dron, until I am dead. And that may be longer than you think."

"Enough of this," said Zef-Dron harshly. "Call the witnesses forward, swear the War Oath, and let us get on with this business."

The witnesses apparently were the warriors from the other five towers. There was no need to call them forward, since they had started out across the Plain of War the moment they saw the argument between the two commanders. Within a few minutes some three hundred warriors in five different colors were assembling in the five different sections of the Plain reserved for the witnesses. With one exception they made no attempt to keep any sort of rigid formation, but sat or stood or even lay about like picnickers rather than warriors.

The exception was the forty-odd warriors in yellow orange. Their section had been marked by a fanged and snarling leopard's head, and they sat in two neat lines. Pen-Jerg looked at them and grunted.

"Those damned Leopards. They know they can make the rest of us look silly just by sitting that way. And it makes our warriors nervous when they go up against the Leopards. That's why the Leopards win almost all the time. If they didn't, they'd be finished. All that playing around with the Peace Wisdom they do. Would you believe that they even let Low People rise to high rank?"

Blade kept his mouth shut and managed to look politely horror-stricken. But he made a mental note that getting in touch with the Tower of the Leopard was a high-priority item. If they were in fact less rule-bound and class-ridden than the other Towers of Melnon—

He was interrupted by a sharp order from Pen-Jerg. "Take your place, Blade."

"Where, Pen-Jerg?"

A grim smile broke Pen-Jerg's sober expression. "If you can defeat Kir-Noz, perhaps we should give you the chance to prove Zef-Dron full of wind. Would you like to be a line leader?"

Blade could not really say that he *did* like the idea. But on the other hand, it was certainly the best way to prove himself. Just as long as there weren't too many warriors as good as Kir-Noz.

He nodded.

"Good. Take the lead of the third line."

Blade fought back the temptation to throw Pen-Jerg a mocking salute. Instead he turned silently and headed for his assigned place in the rapidly assembling formation of the Serpents' warriors.

CHAPTER SIX

Once they had received the proper orders, the warriors of the two towers no longer straggled, stumbled, or delayed. They scurried about like energetic ants, moving into their positions in well-disciplined silence. Within five minutes both sides were lined up and ready, in four lines of ten men each. The two commanders stood off to Blade's right, staring at each other and at each other's formations.

When they had satisfied themselves that everything at least looked ready, both turned to the witnesses from the other towers. "Hail, witnesses," they shouted in unison. "We, commanders of the towers fighting war this day, call on you to witness that each has present on the Plain of War forty chosen and fit warriors and a commander, according to the War Wisdom."

"We so witness!" shouted several dozen voices.

"We rejoice in your witnessing," the two commanders shouted. "We shall now swear the commander's oath."

"I (and here each said his name) swear by the War Wisdom of Melnon, the Peace Wisdom of Melnon, and my own honor, to uphold all laws and customs that govern the war upon this day, the twelfth of the month of the Ox. I swear to slay any man under my command who holds not to these laws and customs. I ask that I myself be slain if I fail in this wise or in myself upholding and obeying that which governs the wars of the Towers of Melnon." A pause for breath. "Do you witness that we have sworn the Commanders' Oath?"

"We so witness!" came again from many of the watchers.

"Is there your consent that we begin the war?"

"There is!" this time coming from nearly all the spectators in a single roar.

Both Pen-Jerg and Zef-Dorn turned to their warriors. "Line leaders—are you ready?"

Blade joined seven other warriors in a single shout of "We are ready!" He found himself having to fight off the notion that this was some sort of religious ritual, that there was not really going to be any fighting or any danger. He knew things were quite different, but it was hard to accept this stylized situation as dangerous or even warlike. He shook his head. After fifteen generations of this sort of flight from reality, the warriors of the Towers of Melnon would be swept away like mice by cats if they ever came up against a realistic and efficient opponent.

The two commanders exchanged a final look. Then each turned back to his warriors and shouted:

"Let the war begin!"

And the line leaders on each side strode forward into the fifty-foot space between the war parties.

Blade came out with a slow sidling step, already dropped into a fighter's crouch, long sword raised to strike, short sword raised to guard. His opponent, half a head shorter than he was but just as broad, strode out without taking any such precautions. As they closed, Blade could see a grim smile on the man's face. Obviously he expected that a man fighting almost naked, and so nervous that he apparently could not stand straight, would be an easy opponent. That was one thing Blade knew he would never be—an easy opponent.

They were twenty feet apart when Blade's opponent dropped into fighting stance. But he did so with an almost negligent air, as if to indicate that he didn't really need to deploy all his skills to defeat Blade. Blade's own face creased in a brief smile. An opponent this overconfident could be easy meat.

Blade let the Eagle warrior launch the first attack. The man came in fast, feinting at Blade's head with the short sword. At the same time the long sword came round in a horizontal slash. It was meant to slice in under Blade's raised guard and chop him nearly in half.

Instead Blade's own short sword darted down like a snake's tongue, warding off the long sword. Steel met steel with a terrible clang. For a moment the other's right arm was frozen by the shock. In that moment Blade's left arm twisted, sending his short sword grating up the long sword, driving point-first into the man's unprotected thigh. His own long sword swung overhand, smashed down through the desperate lunge of the other's short sword, and crashed down on the white helmet. The blow did not penetrate, but it stunned quite thoroughly. Blade stepped back as the Eagle warrior toppled forward on to his face with a resounding thud. From the man's first attack to his last twitch, the whole bout had lasted barely thirty seconds.

Blade was aware of a good many snake-like hisses of indrawn breath from the Serpents behind him. And he saw a good many eyes open wide among the Eagles and the witnesses. But he had no time to care about the audience. His next opponent was stepping forward into the open, looking somewhat nervously at the line leader's prostrate form. But he got himself under control, and signalled to Blade that they should carry the line leader out of the fighting area. With Blade at the head and the other at the feet, they did this. Then they squared off against each other, both in the standard crouch.

The second Eagle warrior was perhaps not so competent as the first. But he lasted longer, because this lack of competence kept him from rushing straight in to his doom like Blade's first opponent had. He stood on the defensive instead, and Blade eventually had to attack and smash down the man's guard in half a dozen quick exchanges. On his seventh long sword blow, Blade struck the Eagle hard

44

enough on the right shoulder to lay open the armor and the flesh beneath it. Blood spurted, then the man dropped both swords on the ground and bowed his head in submission. Blade motioned him aside and waited for the third man.

The third warrior was the biggest warrior Blade had yet seen in Melnon. He must have stood six feet eight, and he was broadly built. But he was also slow in proportion to his bulk, and apparently the slowness extended all the way up from his feet to his wits. He had no ideas for dealing with Blade except to charge in like a mad bull, trying to knock Blade's guard down and his head off by sheer brute strength. This he did so fiercely and so persistently that Blade eventually had to kill him with a thrust in the exposed throat above the neck of his armor. Blood gushed all over the white armor and over the trampled ground. The man gurgled, choked, and swayed. Blade stepped back in time to watch him crash to the ground.

It took two warriors from each side to lug the huge corpse off to the sidelines. The spectacle apparently so preyed on the mind of Blade's next opponent that he considered himself doomed the moment he stepped out to meet Blade. He made no effort to defend himself or even launch an intelligent attack. Instead he charged straight at Blade, screaming at the top of his lungs, waving both swords like the arms of a windmill, determined to at least die spectacularly.

He did not even succeed in doing that. Blade saw at once that this fourth opponent was hardly more than a boy. He certainly didn't want to kill him, and he even preferred to take chances himself to avoid this. Blade dropped down on one knee as the boy closed. He did this so suddenly that the attacker's strokes both whistled through the air where Blade's head had been. Then, before the boy could recover, Blade's own swords darted up. He was gambling on his own speed and sure eye, aiming at precariously small targets—the other man's wrists. Blade's aim was perfect. Both his swords drove into their targets, and both his opponent's swords went flying. Blade jerked a thumb at them, indicating to the boy that he should pick them up and get out of the way. Then he smiled.

"Don't panic, the next time," he said to the boy. "You'll live longer almost any other way. And I think you'll live to be a fine warrior for the Eagles someday—if you're sensible."

The boy stared at Blade with eyes so wide that Blade felt uneasy for a moment. Had he violated the War Wisdom in some way? Then he realized that the boy was trying to hold back tears, which were unfit for a warrior of the Towers of Melnon.

"Thank you, line leader," he said in a strangled voice. Then he bent, retrieved his swords, and stumbled off to the sidelines.

The fifth man was easy, so easy that Blade wondered if the man had deliberately thrown away the fight to save himself wounds or death or captivity. The sixth tried harder, but no more successfully. Eventually Blade closed with him in a *corps à corps* as classic as he could manage with the two curved swords. His knee went up into the man's groin. As the man doubled up and crumpled, Blade slammed the flat of his sword across the back of the man's neck. This time Blade chose to exercise his right to capture the man, who would then have to be ransomed by the Tower of the Eagle for whatever sum in goods or Low People the Tower of the Serpent might set.

As his comrades behind him in the third line led the prisoner off, Blade noticed a look of something like awe in the eyes of several of them. He shrugged. Perhaps he had shown endurance, but he hadn't needed that much skill— yet. His opponents had so far been either inept, half-paralyzed with terror, or overconfident. Sooner or later he was going to meet an Eagle as good as Kir-Noz, who was none of these things.

The seventh man was not that good, although he was the best opponent Blade had met so far in the war. He was fast, completely unintimidated by what he had seen Blade do already, and exceedingly strong. He conducted a very effective defense with arms that were lightning-fast and as strong as the branches of an oak tree. They kept his own swords between his body and Blade's strokes for a long time. So long, in fact, that Blade began to become worried. His opponents were coming to the war completely fresh except for the walk from their tower. He on the other hand had the long and wearing fight with Kir-Noz behind him. He might be able to beat each one of the ten men in the Eagles' third line individually, but the ten of them together might be too much for his endurance.

Fortunately, Blade had no trouble outlasting his seventh opponent. He kept slashes and thrusts coming at the man continuously, from all directions, at all intervals, and at all speeds. Eventually it was a slow thrust with the long sword that found an opening in the man's guard. The tip of Blade's long sword drove into his mouth, and he reeled back, spitting blood and teeth. For a moment shock and pain caused him to drop his guard, and Blade thrust low into his thigh. Blood gushed down the man's leg, and he dropped his swords, knowing that he had lost too much speed to have any hope of coping with Blade's next attack. Blade was not entirely sure of that, so he willingly let the man stumble back to the side of his own tower.

The interval between opponents was longer this time, and Blade had a chance to check on the progress of the War on either side of him. In the fourth line, to his left, Eagles and Serpents were both only on their third fighter. Apparently the two Towers were almost perfectly matched in that line, because the score seemed to be one victory apiece.

In the second line, immediately to Blade's right, the Serpents had a definite edge. Here also they were only on their third warrior, but the Eagles had been forced to bring up their fifth. Before Blade could discover what was going on in the first line, to the far right, his own eighth opponent strode forward.

Blade's trained eye immediately picked this one as the

most dangerous yet. If the Eagles were going to put into the war against him anybody as good as Kir-Noz, this was most likely the man.

The warrior came out slowly, steadily, his eyes never leaving Blade's face but with both swords in position even before he was in the open. Blade did the same. And he did not go straight in to the attack as he had done before. He dropped into a defensive crouch, and began a slow circling around the other man. The other did the same, and they circled slowly around each other three times in succession. Each kept his eyes fixed on the other, searching for any clues to the other's weaknesses. Blade hoped to find some hint of overconfidence or nervousness in the other's expression, but he could not. This man was as sure of his war skills as Blade himself. And he was far fresher than Blade, who was conscious of the sweat pouring off him, the aches in his legs and arms, and the tightness across his chest. He could not hope for luck with this opponent, and for the first time he wished he had insisted on being properly armored. Even if the other wanted only to defeat or capture Blade, it would be hard to keep those razor-sharp swords away from his flesh entirely.

Suddenly, with no wind-up or warning, flat-footed and quick as lightning, the other man struck. Blade plotted the path of the incoming swords and had his own up to meet them in a split-second, but even that was barely in time. The long sword whistled down past Blade's ear, and only a frantic twisting of his body kept it from slashing into his arm. As he twisted he thrust low with his short sword, but the thrust also missed its mark, driving harmlessly into the other man's armored flank.

Around and around the two men went in a succession of deadly circles. They were no longer sizing each other up, for each knew that he would require all his strength and skill to survive, let alone to win. As they circled, they slashed and thrust and parried in a continuous flashing and clanging of steel. And as the swordplay went on and on, Blade became more and more worried. He could not break through this man's guard, nor could he hope to keep up his own guard for much longer. The man was too fast and strong, and Blade knew that he himself was tiring rapidly. If he slowed down, he would be finished.

Blade began recalling details of the fight with Kir-Noz, considering whether that offered any clues to his present situation. He would have no advantage in footwork, and no easy way to make his opponent stumble. Here on the Plain of War the Eagle warrior was fighting on the kind of flat surface where his boots were at their best.

Nor could Blade use his unarmed combat skills. That would no doubt be a violation of the War Wisdom, and put an end to any hope he might have of rising in the Towers of Melnon. That was too bad, for the warriors of Melnon obviously had precious little understanding of unarmed combat. He could surprise his opponent thoroughly with a few karate blows, perhaps thoroughly enough to gain a decisive advantage. But that was impossible.

Or was it? A man disarmed was apparently at the mercy of the victor, to be killed, captured, or released at his discretion. Suppose a man was disarmed and would not submit, but wanted to go on fighting. The logic of the War Wisdom seemed to be to equalize the risks as much as possible for both men and both towers. But if a man deliberately threw away any chance of equality . . .? Blade wished he knew more about the fine points of the War Wisdom. He would like to be sure that there was nothing in his line of reasoning that was leading him into disastrous violations of the Wisdom. But he could hardly call "time out" while he consulted with Pen-Jerg. He flashed a brief glance toward the Serpents' Commander, who was standing where he had been since the beginning of the war. His face was as expressionless as a stone, but Blade noticed a thin sheen of sweat on it that seemed to come from more than the heat of the sun.

Blade turned back to the fight, and made his decision. He would have to gamble, little as he liked the prospect. And he would have to be as subtle as possible, to avoid the risk of trouble over the War Wisdom. He mentally consigned the War Wisdom and all of its votaries to whatever devils might be, then settled down to wait for an opening for his plan. He hoped it would come before too long. He would need all the speed and strength he had left to carry it out.

Fortunately his opponent was also beginning to slow down. Not enough to give Blade any hope of getting through his guard with a sword, but enough to give Blade an extra split-second here and there. Hopefully that would be enough. It had damned well better be!

The man came in again, and again, and a third time. The fourth time, Blade saw the right combination of strokes coming in, the one he had been waiting for. He had both his own swords guarding but held slightly downward as the other's blows descended.

A double-barreled *clang!* Blade opened both hands, and let the other's swords whistle down past him, smashing his own weapons to the ground. They hit with dull thuds and lay there. The other man looked at them, then up at Blade's face, finding no signs of yielding in it.

But the War Wisdom was explicit. "Do you yield yourself as my prisoner?" the man said. He managed to keep some of the triumph out of his voice, but he was clearly pleased with himself. Blade could imagine what honor it would bring the warrior, to have deprived the Tower of the Serpent of such a mighty fighting man.

Blade bared his teeth in a defiant grin. "Not at all, my friend. You will have my corpse or nothing—unless of course I have yours."

It took the warrior a moment to recover from his surprise. Like Kir-Noz, he stared gape-mouthed, as though Blade had suddenly turned into some strange animal. Then he shook his head. "Are you sure, warrior? I would not dishonor you, not after such a fight as you have made. You would be admitted to ransom with small trouble."

"No doubt," said Blade. "Let us agree that *I* chose death

50

before even honorable capture. And then let us see if you can take my body home to the Tower of the Eagle, or if I take yours to the Tower of the Serpent."

The man shook his head again, as though he had to deal with a madman. He could not refuse to continue to fight, but he obviously did not want to. Blade felt a moment's regret at using his plan on this man, but it passed as the man came in again. His long sword rose high, then came whistling down, aiming at Blade's head, seeking to split it open like a melon.

As the sword came down Blade dropped into a crouch. Then he sprang out of it, toward the man and under the descending sword. He felt it sear his shoulder, but as it did so his balled left fist drove hard into the man's face. The warrior's head snapped back and for a moment he forgot that he still held the short sword in a position where he could easily drive it into Blade's side.

That moment was all Blade needed to crash his opponent's left arm, twist it at the wrist, and heave. The Eagle warrior sailed up and over Blade's shoulder in a perfect judo throw. He hit the ground with a crash that knocked all the wind out of him and knocked both swords out of his hands. Before he could recover either his breath or his weapons Blade was kneeling on his chest, both hands clamped behind the man's neck. The smallest jerk by his powerful arms would have snapped the fallen man's neck like a carrot. And the man saw that clearly. As his breath came back his lips began to move soundlessly. Finally he grated out two words.

"I yield."

Blade grinned like a death's-head. "That is well. For I do not want to kill you either. Rise, take your swords, and return to the lines of the Tower of the Eagle."

It took the man a moment to realize that Blade was actually letting him go. When he did, it seemed to restore all his strength in an instant. He sprang up as though he had been lying on an ant nest, snatched up both his swords, and lurched back to his own side as fast as his legs would carry him. Blade retrieved his own weapons and squatted on his heels, watching and waiting for his ninth opponent to come out. He could not help hoping that the remaining men in the Eagles' third line were either boys or old men. He did not feel strong enough to fight anything else.

The ninth man was coming out now, and so was the tenth. Side by side they walked out toward Blade, and side by side they stopped and threw their swords down on the ground. As they did that, shouts and cries rose from the warriors of both towers. They were cries of amazement from the Eagles' warriors, and of delight and triumph from the Serpents'. Even the Serpents' wounded were cheering.

Commander Zef-Dron stepped forward, shaking his head as if he could not believe what he had just seen. He stepped up to Pen-Jerg, and in a loud clear voice said, "Pen-Jerg, I declare that the Eagles yield in this day's war. The Tower of the Serpent is the victor." He shook his head again, and went on less formally, "I can hardly believe it. Eight Eagles defeated by this warrior, and two more who refuse to fight him. And to think—I thought he would be sliced to pieces by his first opponent." Zef-Dron shook his head once more, then turned back to his men. "Release the Serpent prisoners and gather up our dead and wounded. It is time to return to our tower."

The Eagles did not seem interested in waiting around. In silence, with stunned and bewildered faces, they obeyed their Commander's orders. Within a few minutes their line was marching away across the Plain, toward the great white bulk of their tower looming beyond. Only the scufflings and scarrings of the Plain and the blood already half-dried in the sun showed that there had been a war.

The Serpents and the witnesses had watched in silence also, as if Blade's feat had also numbed and stunned them. As the Eagles tramped away, the witnesses rose also and began to drift away toward their edges of the Plain. Blade watched the well-drilled contingent from the Tower of the Leopard particularly closely. They at least seemed to want to linger. Only reluctantly did they form two perfectly-dressed lines and march away, keeping perfect cadence and chanting to themselves.

The departure of the Leopards was like a signal to the Serpents. In a pandemonium of cheering and screaming all who could walk surged forward. They swarmed around Blade, and he felt dozens of hands clutching at him, lifting him, hoisting him high. For a moment he wondered if he was going to be torn apart by his own friends after surviving all the day's fighting.

Then the crowd spread out. Blade found himself straddling the shoulders of two of the largest warriors, and balanced unright by the hands of a dozen more. The cheering swelled again as he rose into view.

Then Pen-Jerg's booming voice beat down the cheers. "Warriors of the Tower of the Serpent. Hail the new warrior of the First Rank—Blade!"

The cheers this time were loud enough to make Blade want to put his hands over his ears.

CHAPTER SEVEN

The warriors of the Tower of the Serpent carried Blade on their shoulders all the way back through the Waste Lands to the base of the tower. That was just as well. Exhaustion, release of tension, and loss of blood from his wounded shoulder were making him light-headed. But his head was not so fogged that he wasn't able to do some hasty thinking.

It was hardly more than noon of his first day in the dimension of the Towers of Melnon. Yet he had already won acceptance as a warrior of one of the towers, a warrior of the First Rank in fact. He had a name, a reputation, a status, the friendship or at least the support of two other prominent warriors of the Tower of the Serpent, and the prestige that came from almost single-handedly winning a war for his new tower. From what the shouting warriors said as they carried him along, Blade gathered that this was something done perhaps once in a generation, if that often. He was doing well enough for the moment.

For the moment. He didn't have any idea of the possible dangers of his situation. Nor could he, until he learned a good deal more about life inside the Tower of the Serpent. And other Towers as well, he added to himself. Particularly the Tower of the Leopard. That Tower of well-drilled warriors looked and sounded worth investigating, if he ever had the opportunity to do so safely. But he didn't even know whether there was any peaceful contact among the Towers on a day-to-day basis. He decided to stop worrying about the future and enjoy the hero's reception that no doubt waited for him in the Tower of the Serpent.

He was not disappointed. Pen-Jerg must have sent messengers on ahead with word of Blade's epic triumph. As the war party lumbered across the Waste Land, Blade could see the balcony on the side toward him turning almost solid green with people. The lifters were going up and down almost continuously as well, lowering others to the ground. More than two hundred warriors were waiting at the base of the tower by the time the war party and Blade arrived. They greeted him with a new outburst of cheering. Blade found that his head was beginning to ache. It was a relief when they lowered him to the ground and stood around him. It would have been more of a relief if they had stood back and given him a chance to breathe.

Blade could hear Pen-Jerg bellowing, "What? The wounded man's lifter not down yet? Didn't Queen Mir-Kasa order it? What! You're suggesting that Her Splendor hasn't thought of everything for greeting a hero! Why you—" which led to a very detailed description of somebody's habits, ancestry, and likely fate. It was followed by an equally detailed description of Blade's heroism. No doubt Pen-Jerg intended it to make whoever had interfered with the reception for Blade feel even more like a worm than before. The description went on for nearly five minutes, occasionally interrupted by still more outbursts of cheering. It ended only when Pen-Jerg apparently ran out of breath. Blade had the impression that Pen-Jerg liked to play to a good audience if he could find one. No doubt such nearly perfect occasions were rare.

Red-faced and perspiring, the Commander then pushed his way through the warriors gathered around Blade and stood over him, looking down at him. Blade decided to use the time until the lifter arrived to ask a few more questions.

"What happens now, Pen-Jerg?"

The commander took a deep breath. "The wounded man's

lifter will be sent down for you. It should have been here already, but that—"

"I know," put in Blade. "I heard you describing him. In fact, I suspect they heard you describing him at the top of the Tower of the Eagle."

Pen-Jerg grinned. "Perhaps they did. But to speak of you—you will ride up to the balcony in the lifter. Then we will lead you to the warrior's shaft, and up to the reception chamber. Queen Mir-Kasa will greet you there. I think Nris-Pol—" He broke off there, as if he had decided what he was going to say about Nris-Pol was not fit for public consumption. "But the queen will greet you, and confirm your status as a warrior of the First Rank, and give you a name of honor among the High People of the Tower of the Serpent. But before that, you must also have a common name in the style of Melnon. What was your mother's name?"

"Why do you ask that?"

"It is very simple. A man or woman belongs to the family of their mother. Each person has a name of his own—a birth name—joined with the name of his mother. I, for example, am birth-named Pen, while my mother's name was Jerga. Thus I am Pen-Jerg. Our queen's mother, queen before her, was Kasa, and named her daughter Mir. So now we are ruled by Queen Mir-Kasa.

Blade nodded, and decided against asking any questions about kings. He doubted if there would be any such thing, and even asking about them might be considered—well, disagreeable. At least in the Tower of the Serpent they were matrilineal—that is, descent was traced through the mother. They might even be completely matriarchal—ruled by women. If that was the case, the warriors might be only a subordinate caste, and their rule-bound wars would make more sense. The Council of Wisdom could be—

Blade reined himself in sharply. He was not an anthropologist, although he had lived and loved and fought among people that any of a thousand anthropologists would have sold their souls to observe. And even anthropologists were not supposed to let their guesses run along ahead of the facts this way. There was a more immediate problem—his name.

"My mother's name was Elizabeth," he said.

"A terribly long name," said Pen-Jerg. "No doubt we can arrange to have it written down properly in the Book of Honor and elsewhere that the scribes insist. But to call you by it every moment of your life—can we shorten it to Liza, perhaps?"

"All right."

"Good. You will be something-Liza. What does the word 'bla-hayd' mean in English?"

Blade grinned. "It means a sharp cutting tool. Like a sword, for example."

Pen-Jerg stared for a moment, then burst out in roars of delighted laughter. "That is almost too perfect to believe. I cannot think of a better name of honor for you than 'sword.' But your name already means something like that in your own tongue. So you shall be known both among the warriors and in the Book of Honor as Blade-Liza. Do you consent?"

"I do."

Blade didn't see that he had much choice in the matter, in any case. And he noted that Pen-Jerg was quietly accepting his story of coming from a strange people called the English. Apparently now that he had proved he could do things according to the War Wisdom, no one was disposed to argue over where he came from. One more point settled in his favor. But there was something else to mention.

"Pen-Jerg, is there going to be such a thing as a doctor to treat me? That eighth man did give me something of a gash in the shoulder. Or hasn't anybody noticed?" There was a sarcastic ring to his voice as he said the last sentence.

A moment later he regretted it. "Why, of course," said Pen-Jerg. "A surgeon will indeed come to you—perhaps even the First Surgeon. We all saw the wound. But you said nothing of it, so we assumed that you were choosing to ignore it, in the manner of true heroes."

"And I shall continue to ignore it," said Blade firmly. "It has stopped bleeding"—largely true—"and it no longer pains me greatly"—which was definitely not true. "But even heroes can die or become unable to fight for their towers if they are careless about wounds altogether. So let the surgeon do his best." Blade wasn't sure if he was going to lose any of his hero's position by saying this. But he knew he would a damned sight rather be less heroic and alive than more heroic and dead from an untreated and infected wound!

Before Pen-Jerg had any time to reply a shout came over the crowd that the wounded man's lifter was ready. Instead of the flying-trapeze arrangement of the regular lifters, it was a large rectangular mesh basket, with a padded bottom. A "wounded man" could stand, sit, or lie in it, depending on the seriousness of his wound and his own inclinations. Blade decided to sit. He would not cut so fine a figure sitting on the cushions as he would standing tall. But he was not sure if he could keep his balance as the basket swayed up the two hundred feet to the balcony. He had visions of himself striking a dramatic pose, overbalancing, and toppling out of the basket to drop all the way to the ground. That would end both of his careers—his permanent one and his new temporary one as a warrior of the Tower of the Serpent.

He climbed into the basket, braced himself against the mesh, and nodded. High above somebody shouted, and the basket lurched and swayed up into the air. Close up, Blade could see that it was raised and lowered on two incredibly thin cords or wires attached to swivel shackles at either end. No doubt the regular lifters used the same. That cord would be worth examining. It appeared to be hardly thicker than heavy sewing thread, yet two strands of it were raising Blade, lifter, and all, a total weight of several hundred pounds. Possibly more, for the frame of the lifter was made of solid metal rods at least an inch thick.

The lifter sailed rapidly up towards the balcony. As it approached the top, Blade saw hundreds of faces begin to line the railing, peering down at him. Up here he could see both men and women in the crowd—apparently the women were forbidden on the ground. The men were mostly wearing warriors' clothing, although some wore long flowing green robes and broad-brimmed hats. The women wore green also, but they were mostly bare-headed, and no two of their robes or gowns seemed to follow the same pattern. Blade saw everything from voluminous wrappings that covered and concealed from neck to ankles to abbreviated tunics that covered no more than a short nightgown and were semitransparent to boot.

The lifter reached the edge of the balcony, and once more eager hands by the dozen reached down to help Blade out. Looking up, he saw that, about thirty feet up, narrow catwalks ran out from small doors in the tower to the very edge of the balcony. At the end of each catwalk was a large winch, and at each winch sat a naked man, head shaved and chained by one ankle to the catwalk railing. As Blade watched, one of them began turning the handle of his winch. One of the trapeze lifters, hanging from the end of the catwalk, dropped slowly toward the level of the balcony. When it had reached that level, a man in warriors' gear was waiting there, to step gracefully into it and drop out of sight clinging to it.

As the warrior dropped out of sight, the men and women on the balcony crowded around Blade, exclaiming over his appearance, his wounds, and other things that made Blade almost want to blush. Frankness, it seemed, was a virtue—or at least not frowned on—in the Towers of Melnon. Then once more a crowd gave way before Pen-Jerg's bull strength and bull voice. The warrior reached down a hand to Blade and hauled him to his feet. "Enough of this!" he bellowed. "You'll get a chance to admire him and ask him all the questions you want at his Honor Naming. For the moment, he's Queen Mir-Kasa's business."

"Particularly what he's got between his legs!" shouted one woman. "When the queen gets one look at that, she'll never let him go!"

"I wonder how Nris-Pol's going to like that?" said a warrior, and answered himself with a coarse laugh.

"Enough, you babbling fools!" snapped Pen-Jerg. His face was flushed and red with more than his exertions. Obviously he did not like public discussion of bedroom politics. Neither did Blade. He kept his mouth shut as Pen-Jerg led him across the balcony, through the crowd, and into the Tower of the Serpent.

A long corridor ran in from the door, zigzagging sharply toward the center of the tower. It was almost completely deserted except for an occasional warrior who seemed to be on guard. But there were occasional polished metal grills in the wall. Blade could see pale, sunken-eyed faces framed in long dark hair staring through these grills.

"What is beyond those walls?" he asked Pen-Jerg, pointing.

"Nothing that need concern you—I hope," said Pen-Jerg, with emphasis on that last two words. "Merely a level of the quarters of the Low People. It were more in keeping with the Peace Wisdom that we High People did not have to pass through their levels of the tower even as little as we do. But when the towers were built the Peace Wisdom and the War Wisdom were both for the future, and the reels and lifters not as good as they are today. It was considered both fit and wise to build the balcony where it is. And none have ever seen fit to move it higher."

"How far up would it have to be moved?"

"The levels of the Low People and the work chambers extend up perhaps three times higher than this," replied Pen-Jerg. "If the balcony were moved, we would have less to do with the Low People. And it would improve the breed of warriors. There are some weaklings among us now who can ride the lifters down from the present balcony. But were it thrice as far above the Waste Land, their weak hearts would show themselves."

Blade could not help feeling that it was just as well the balcony was at its present height. He did not particularly look forward to playing the daring young man on the flying trapeze even at a mere two hundred feet up. Six or eight hundred feet up the sheer side of the tower, he suspected his own "weak heart" might show itself.

They reached a corridor that curved away to the left and the right, and took it to the left. When they came to a door decorated with the figure of a warrior in full armor, both swords drawn, Pen-Jerg stopped. Then he pressed a button beside the door. It slid open, and he motioned Blade through.

Inside was a large circular chamber entirely decorated in more pastel shades of green. As Blade looked around, he felt the floor under him quiver, and the chamber started moving upward. It rose so fast that he had to swallow hard several times to clear his ears. Pen-Jerg looked at him and smiled. "Yes, the Shaft of the Warriors rises the fastest of all the shafts in the Tower of the Serpent. And the shafts of the Tower of the Serpent rise the fastest among all the shafts of all the Towers of Melnon. Do you have such things in England, Blade-Liza?"

"Indeed we do," said Blade. He was a trifle surprised at Pen-Jerg's boasting. The spirit in which the people of the towers seemed to go off to war was more like that of a football game than an army. No, that wasn't the best analogy, considering how many football and soccer games had turned into riots much bloodier than the war he had just fought. In any case, Pen-Jerg's remark suggested that beneath the surface of fairness and even temper the rivalries among the towers aroused strong feelings.

By the time Blade had finished considering this; the elevator car was slowing down. Finally it stopped, and the door swished open. A reception committee was waiting for them in the chamber outside—a warrior, white-haired and stooping, and two men in the flowing robes and broad hats of civilians. Both wore badges pinned to the brims of their hats—one appeared to be a gilded pen, the other a gilded vial.

"You are honored, Blade-Liza," said Pen-Jerg. "The First Warrior, the First Scribe, and the First Surgeon of the Tower of the Serpent are all here to receive you and prepare you for Queen Mir-Kasa. This is an additional honor that I had not expected even for you."

Blade was not sure how to react, so he contented himself with a bow as deep as he could manage. That appeared to be enough. The three men returned his bow, and led him and Pen-Jerg into a chamber beyond. This one was furnished with luxurious couches, a sunken bath with every imaginable extra, and a large desk. The First Scribe sat down at the desk, opened a plate in the corner of the top, and unfolded a small microphone on a long boom. Then he pressed a button, and lights flashed on all over the top of the desk.

"Speak toward this recorder, Blade-Liza. To take down your account of who you are and what you have done this way is not our custom. Normally a person being presented to Her Splendor has all the details of his life already recorded in the Metal Mind. But you are from—let us say, someplace other than the Towers of Melnon. There is much that we would know of one from our own Tower that we do not know of you. And without its being known, we cannot be altogether sure that you are fit to meet Queen Mir-Kasa or receive any honors or status among us. Speak, Blade-Liza. The First Surgeon will attend your wounds while you do. Then there will be food and drink for you."

Blade nodded. Apparently there *were* a few more hurdles to get over before his status among these people would be secure. Well, he should have expected it. And at least he came from a profession where lying with a straight face was a survival skill you learned early—or you didn't live to learn it afterward. He had both offered and broken cover stories a good deal more difficult than anything he was likely to need with these people.

Out of the corner of his eye he saw the First Surgeon laying out his instruments and dressings on one of the couches. He cleared his throat, and began.

"My name is Richard Blade, Blade-Liza among the people of the Towers of Melnon. I was born in England, in—"

CHAPTER EIGHT

Blade talked into the microphone for the better part of an hour. Sometimes he had to stop and grit his teeth at the pain as the surgeon probed his wound, or smeared salve over it, or took stitches in the flesh with what felt like a sail-maker's needle. But the man seemed to know his business, and at the end of the hour the wound was cleaned, stitched up, bandaged, and no longer hurting much.

Blade managed to get through that entire hour's interrogation by the First Scribe without any obvious slips. He played his cards very close to his chest, volunteering no information, and answering only the most direct questions as briefly as possible. But he had to be careful there, since answering too briefly would be likely to arouse suspicion. Admittedly the First Scribe seemed fairly unsophisticated and unsuspicious, for all his rank. But Blade was too familiar with the range of poses a trained interrogator could take to trust any of them on outward signs.

He was also very careful to say as little as possible about English methods of war or the organization of English society. Those seemed to be the two areas where people in Melnon were most likely to cry heresy and try to burn you at the stake—or at least send you down among the Low People. When the topics did come up, Blade tried to give the impression that he really hadn't been especially happy with the way things were in England. In fact, he implied that he

64

was very happy to have finally arrived where society was properly organized and fought its wars the way he had always wanted to fight. Again he had to be careful, since he didn't want to show more enthusiasm than he could make sound authentic. But he managed to keep a straight face, and the First Scribe showed no signs of suspicion.

If answering questions about the "Low People" of England was ticklish, asking about the "Low People" of the towers was even more so. Blade kept his mouth entirely shut on that subject, as much as he would have liked to learn more about it. But luck was with him again. Before he left the recreation chamber, he had learned a good deal about the relative position of High and Low in at least the Tower of the Serpent. Much of it he needed to know, but would never have dared ask. However, the method of learning it left something to be desired.

By the time the interrogation was completed, Blade's throat was dry. He asked for a drink.

"Certainly," said the First Warrior. "What is your desire? We have water, wine, *fujol, wolmnas*—" going on to list about twenty names. Blade supposed they were all things to drink, but they made as much sense to him as if they had all been in medieval Sanskrit. He held up a hand to stop the flow of hospitality.

"Water will be fine," he said. He wanted a clear head if he was going before Queen Mir-Kasa. Almost as important, it was harder to slip drugs or poisons into water than into something that might conceal their taste with its own. No doubt a psychiatrist sitting in some paneled office in London would call this attitude paranoid. Blade preferred to think of it as common-sense survival.

The First Warrior nodded. "Again, you show the wisdom of a hero. Wine or other strong drinks inflame the blood and slow the healing of wounds. But water purges inner imbalances and speeds the healing. Is that not right, Surgeon?"

"It is."

The First Warrior stepped to the desk and reached over the scribe's shoulder to press a button in a complex rhythm. There was a moment's delay, then a *beep* and a red light that flashed three times. "Your water will come shortly," said the First Warrior. "And I asked that bath servants come also, and a clothing worker. Queen Mir-Kasa may wish to see you as you are, for she cares little for things which stand between her and her curiosity. Such is the nature of women, and of queens. But she may also wish you fitly garbed."

"Indeed," said Blade. It was a word he had found useful in half a dozen different dimensions, to register agreement on topics that he did not entirely understand. But he made yet another mental note. Queen Mir-Kasa sounded like a strong-minded and self-willed woman. Good or bad? No way of telling at the moment.

The various servants called for must have been only a few chambers away, because they arrived less than two minutes later. There were four of them, all women, all naked as babies except for tight-fitting masks over their mouths and noses and elbow-length gloves. In fact, they were quite unnaturally naked. Except for a sort of Indian scalplock, every speck of body hair had been shaved off. And their bare skins glistened unnaturally with some sort of grease or oil with an unmistakably antiseptic smell. Blade found himself looking at them with barely controlled distaste, although all four were young and all four had more than presentable figures.

One of them carried a green enameled tray with a large jug and a small cup on it. The other three carried large sacks that bulged, no doubt, with bathing gear and clothing. Blade rose, stepped up to the water-bearer, and without thinking about it picked up the jug and poured himself a cupful of water.

There was a sudden metallic clatter that made Blade stop with the cup half-way to his lips. The girl had dropped the tray and jug to the floor, and was standing as if turned to stone. Her eyes were wide with unmistakable terror, as they

66

shifted from the spreading wetness on the rug, to Blade, to the First Warrior, and back again. The First Warrior's face also seemed frozen, but his expression was obviously one of almost apoplectic rage. With an effort, he seemed to calm himself and shake his head, more in sorrow than in anger.

"Ah, Blade-Liza, I grieve that the Servant Master should have been so lax as to send such wretched people to wait upon the hero of this day's war. She should have known her people better than this. I will see that she is sent among the Low People for this."

The First Scribe shook his head. "Perhaps it would be better to merely send her to the Pleasure Chamber for a week. Is it reasonable to ask that she should know which servants can be trusted to wait upon Blade-Liza, a man completely unfamiliar with the Peace Wisdom?" He looked severly at Blade. "You should know that no High Person may take anything directly from the hands of one of the Low People. The Low People must always place whatever they bring upon the floor at the High Peoples' feet."

Blade nodded. "I am indeed in many ways ignorant of both your War and your Peace Wisdom. But in that case, why should anyone be punished. If the ignorance is mine, so is the—"

"Silence!" boomed all three of the officials together, in one deafening roar. "If you speak further, it will be necessary to administer to all four of the servants, instead of just the one who is at fault. What you were going to say is forbidden to one of the High People in the presence of any of the Low."

Blade was not entirely sure he understood what he had just done, but decided that the safest course was to keep his mouth shut. It was obvious in any case that he could not save the girl. The First Warrior went on, in a more reasoned tone, "The fault is and must be that of the Low Person. Were she properly trained and obedient to the Peace Wisdom for the Low People, she would never have let you take the cup from the tray. She would have dropped it on the floor before you could do so."

Blade felt compelled to raise an objection, purely on grounds of logic. "But then I would have received no water."

The First Warrior's expression seemed to be hanging between a laugh and a glare. "The Peace Wisdom says nothing about you getting the water. Had she dropped it, she would have been only lightly administered, for soiling the rug. As it is, she will receive the Principal Administration, for without that the Peace Wisdom will be weakened." That seemed to settle the argument as far as the First Warrior was concerned. Blade mentally shrugged his shoulders. He had better resign himself to never finding logic or even common sense in either the War or the Peace Wisdom.

Now the First Warrior stepped toward the offending girl. As he did, the other three girls slowly backed away from her, until she stood alone, still frozen stone-stiff. The First Warrior snatched the mask from her face, then reached down to his belt and unhooked the white wand hanging there, holding it carefully by its silvered end. He lifted it, then pointed it toward the floor. Slowly, as if her joints needed oiling, the girl knelt down, then bowed her neck. The First Warrior stepped up to her, stood over her, and pressed the green end of the wand to the base of her skull.

Instantly the girl's mouth snapped open, and the most appalling scream Blade had ever heard from a human throat tore through the chamber. Blade could not imagine the degree of pain that must be behind that scream. He did not even want to try. The girl began to shake all over, as though she were suffering a violent chill. Her scream continued, though, until there was no more air in her lungs. Then her eyes rolled up in her head, and she fell forward onto the floor, still shaking. The First Warrior kept the wand in place and did not raise it for another minute. By that time the girl's shaking was like the motion of an earthworm cut in two— something Blade had never seen or hoped to see in a human being. When the First Warrior stood up and lifted the wand from the back of her neck, the girl finally stopped moving.

The First Warrior stepped back for a moment, then with a look of infinite distaste on his face he thrust one booted foot under the girl's belly and lifted. She rolled over on her back, as limply as if all her bones had been turned to jelly, and the First Warrior's expression of distaste deepened. So did Blade's.

The girl's eyes were mere blank red pools, from which blood flowed as she turned over. And more blood was trickling from every body opening—ears, nose, mouth, genitals. The blackness of bleeding under the skin stood out vividly in her temples, wrists, ankles, breasts, and groin.

The First Warrior looked sourly at the blood trickling out onto the immaculate green carpet, and shook his head. "I am getting sadly out of practice, Blade-Liza. I would not have done such an—inefficient—job of Principal Administration a few years ago. Then I could have kept an erring servant girl building slowly toward the final peak for fifteen or twenty minutes, conscious all the while. As it is, I have cause to be ashamed. I shall have to ask for the next few Principal Administrations to be entrusted to me, so that I can regain my touch. Perhaps you would like to help me, Blade-Liza? You will need to learn how to conduct all levels of administration among the Low People if you are to rise as high among us as I think you will.

"Indeed," said Blade. He did not dare say anything more. He could not, without his tone of voice making his true opinions unmistakably clear. The administration he had just seen made him feel sick to his stomach. The thought of having to give administrations himself made him even sicker. Any ideas of asking for food vanished on the instant.

The First Warrior, oblivious to Blade's clenched teeth and quick breath, went about observing the proprieties. He went over to the desk, punched a different rhythm into the signal button, then turned back to the three remaining servants. He raised his hands, pointed at Blade, then made a series of signs in the area. Apparently, there was some taboo about

69

communicating verbally with the Low People. But the girls obviously understood, because they in turn pointed to Blade, then towards the bath. One of them went over to the gilded nozzles at its head and began turning on the water. Another motioned that Blade should take off his sword belt. He did so, stepped over to the bath, and sat down on the marble bottom. The water rose around him, faintly perfumed and exactly the right temperature. He felt the filth and sweat of the day's exertions floating off his body, and the kinks and knots easing out of his over-worked muscles. In fact, he found it hard not to simply drift off to sleep, letting the servant girls do with him what they would.

Abruptly a gong rang out, loud and brazen and booming, the sound rolling through the air of the chamber. All three of the officials jumped a foot in the air and stared at each other in nervous surprise. The servant girls jumped even higher, dropping the soaps and brushes and bottles of oil they were pulling from the bags. One of the bottles broke open as it struck the stone edge of the tub. An almost overpowering smell of perfumed oil filled the air of the chamber.

Blade sat up in the bath. "What the—? What is happening now?"

The First Surgeon was the first of the officials to recover his voice. "Queen Mir-Kasa."

"What about Queen Mir-Kasa? Is she dead, or being crowned, or what?" Blade's impatience showed in his voice.

His commanding tone seemed to restore some of the three men's courage and composure. The First Warrior shrugged as he turned to Blade. "I told you that Her Splendor is a willful woman who lets nothing stand in the way of what she wants."

"So?"

"She is coming here. That gong announces her."

"Yes, she is coming here," repeated the First Scribe. "This is most irregular. You are not properly prepared. We can—"

"I am a damned sight readier than you are!" snapped Blade. He was torn between anger and amusement at the sight of the three sadistic chair-warmers falling all over themselves at Mir-Kasa's apparent violation of custom. "And I suggest that somebody go to the door and let her in. In England it is considered very much against any wisdom to keep a queen waiting outside a door."

CHAPTER NINE

Keeping a queen waiting outside a door was apparently bad form in Melnon as well as in England. At least that was the impression Blade got from the expression on Queen Mir-Kasa's face when the door slid open and she entered.

She was drawn up to her full height as she strode in, her gown swirling about her. She was only an inch or so shorter than Blade's six one. Wide dark eyes blazed as brightly as the gems in the tiara perched in her mass of dark hair, and her full red lips were drawn into a tight line. Two spots of vivid color that were not the result of cosmetics shone on her face. It was a face tanned and unwrinkled, although a good many strands of gray in the queen's hair suggested that she was well past forty. Nor did as much of her body as Blade could see show many signs of age. He could see much of it, for the queen wore a sleeveless form-fitting tunic with a neckline plunging down between her breasts to just above her navel, and a long flowing semitranslucent skirt. More startling than their limited coverage was their color. Instead of the all-pervasive and by now deadly monotonous green, Mir-Kasa wore silver gray shot with red and purple threads, and purple sandals on her slender feet.

Blade had plenty of time to observe the queen, because she stopped just inside the door to glare at the three officials clustered around the desk. Their eyes met hers briefly, then dropped to the floor. A sharp motion of one long-fingered royal hand, and four warriors dressed in the same silver gray as the queen followed her into the chamber and took position on either side of her. She looked in fact like a victorious general entering a conquered town at the head of an army. Blade had the feeling that it would take very little to make her order the four warriors behind her into action.

As if they had read his thoughts, all four of them drew their long swords with a rasp of steel. At this the three officials became even more nervous, if that was possible. The First Scribe reeled and would have actually fallen to the rug if he had not been able to support himself on the desk. Blade noted that the three servant girls now actually seemed less frightened than the three High People.

Mir-Kasa's eyes were fixed entirely on the High People. There was an expression in those eyes that Blade did not like. It was an open, naked, enjoyment of power—particularly the power to inspire terror—a savoring of that power just this side of madness. Blade began to wonder if there was much safety to be gained by the queen's friendship. But on the other hand, if there was nothing to be gained by her enmity except death—?

Eventually Mir-Kasa got tired of making her officials quake in their boots. She made another sharp gesture, and the four warriors sheathed their swords and fell back to stand against the wall with their arms crossed on their chests. Her eyes dropped to the body of the administered girl. She laughed deep in her throat and smiled thinly.

"So that was the delay? A matter of administration only?"

"Yes, Your Splendor. She—" Another waved hand cut the First Warrior off abruptly.

"There is a time and a place for everything, my good servant, as even the War Wisdom says. Administrations can be dealt with at other times and places than this. And so can you. Now depart."

"But—" It was the First Surgeon who mustered up the courage to speak.

"No." Mir-Kasa did not raise her voice, but all three men

flinched at the word. The power-lusting look was back in her eyes. The three saw it as clearly as Blade did, and took the warning. They were out through the door and out of the chamber so fast the First Surgeon did not even pick up his medical kit. A quick gesture from the queen, and the three girls followed them; a nod, and the warriors were gone. The door sighed shut, leaving Blade and the queen of the Tower of the Serpent alone in the chamber.

Blade felt a tension and an arousal that was not entirely erotic, although he strongly suspected what the queen had in mind. Being alone with this woman was a little like being alone with a tame but hungry leopard. He couldn't be sure when the hunger might suddenly overpower the tameness.

"Well, my new warrior of the First Rank. I, Mir-Kasa, greet you."

Blade was not sure whether he should rise naked from the bath, so he contrived to bow sitting half-submerged in the cooling water. The queen laughed. Now that she was no longer trying to intimidate and terrorize, her voice was a rich throaty contralto.

"Do not stand—or sit—upon ceremony with me here—ah?"

"Blade-Liza, Your Splendor."

"Nor call me by my title, either," she added. "I spit upon ceremony whenever I can. And I would spit upon the ceremonious if I could. But even I am not my own mistress—yet. I am told that you come from a land said to lie in the Beyond, Blade-Liza. Is that so?"

"It is."

"The reports that came to me said so. But some of the warriors who follow the Serpent see marvels in anything that is not in the War Wisdom. The more fools they. Do you have such notions among your people, the—English, is that it?"

"I am indeed of the English, and we do have some of that kind of person among us, although we have no War Wisdom quite like yours." Fortunately, Blade added to himself. We have enough trouble fighting wars as it is.

The queen's eyes widened. "No War Wisdom. Then how do you fight your wars?"

Blade started to explain, but the queen held up a hand to command silence. Then her lips curled again, in what Blade could only describe as a lustful grin. He no longer had any doubt as to what she planned to do with their privacy.

"Blade-Liza, I would like to have you by me, as Queen's Steward. That is a post that must be held by a warrior of the First Rank, with—certain other qualities—besides. For the moment it is held by a lout named Nris-Pol—ah, I see you know him. But he wearies me. He is beginning to lose his other qualities. And he was never blessed with very many brains to begin with. So I think I will find out if you are fit to take his place. And then——" She paused for so long that Blade was driven to prompting her.

"And then?"

The queen lowered her voice, as if afraid of being overheard. "And then if you have—qualities—between your ears as well as between your legs, we can move on to other matters. *You* can move on to other matters, such as no man in Melnon has ever touched before."

Mir-Kasa's words were ambiguous, but to Blade's trained ear her tone was not. She had dreams of absolute rule, and of Blade as her consort in that rule. Why would she consider an outsider for such a position? But then—who else but an outsider? He would have no loyalty to the War Wisdom, the Peace Wisdom, the system of High and Low People, or any of the other stifling traditions of the Towers of Melnon. He would be a new broom that she could use to make a clean sweep of all her enemies. Well and good, but not what he would have done by choice. However, when one can only choose between riding the tiger or being eaten by it . . .

Blade nodded, letting his eyes show the rest of what he wanted to say. Mir-Kasa's grin broadened until Blade thought it was going to meet at the back of her head. Then she threw back her head, snatched the tiara off, and dropped it on the rug. Her long dark hair flowed unconfined down her back. It was a very fine back, Blade noticed—as straight and supple as a young girl's. He returned her grin with one of his own.

It was as if the grin had injected her with an aphrodisiac. Her lower lip trembled, and her even white teeth clamped down on it. Her nostrils flared, and Blade saw her breasts heave as she took a deep breath. Then she motioned to him, sharply, almost as if she were angry.

"Come out of that water. No, do not bother to dry yourself off. I want you wet against me, wet. And I want to see how you treat a woman. A woman, Blade, a woman. Not a queen. For now and for all these moments between us forever I am not a queen but a woman with a man. Is that clear?"

If Mir-Kasa's words had not been clear, the look on her face would certainly have been so. To judge from the hunger Blade could see there, the about-to-become-ex-Steward Nris-Pol could have been a eunuch. He doubted whether that was really the case. It was more likely that Her Splendor Mir-Kasa, Queen of the Tower of the Serpent, had rather extensive appetites.

He climbed out of the bath and strode dripping and naked across the carpet, leaving a damp trail behind him. For a moment his eyes fell on the girl's body. If Mir-Kasa was going to insist on making love with that gruesome reminder of the way of life in the towers lying on the rug only feet away . . .

She was. Blade shrugged mentally as she came toward him, eyes half-closed, mouth open. He had made love under less agreeable circumstances, and to far less attractive women. Mir-Kasa's age might be showing in her hair, but Blade could not see it showing anywhere else. The high full breasts thrust out the material of the tunic in solid, firm, unsagging shapes, and the skin of her neck showed only the faintest lining and wrinkling.

Then she was in his arms, her lips clinging hot and wet to his, and Blade knew that both the maturity and the madness in this woman extended deep into her. All by itself, the kiss

76

was an almost frighteningly powerful erotic poem. For a moment Blade had the unnerving sensation that this woman was going to physically suck him in, every inch of his body, and mix herself with him. His arousal almost cooled for a moment at the image. Then he felt her hands moving down his body, not waiting for any subtle caresses. They went straight to his up-jutting maleness and went to work on it with the same fierce intensity. A momentary thought flashed through Blade's mind, that his maleness was going to be up-jetting before too much longer with this kind of handwork. And then where would he be? Not Queen's Steward of the Tower of the Serpent, that was certain.

As her hands flickered around him, his own were searching up and down her body, squeezing, caressing as best he could through the clothes. He was also looking for ways of taking those clothes off, for there was a rutting madness boiling up in him. He wanted her as bare to him and his hands as he was to her.

Her garments seemed to be made without buttons, hooks, zippers, fasteners, or openings of any sort. For a moment doubt flickered through his mind. Was he supposed to tear the clothes off the back of a queen? Then another thought came into his mind and stayed there. If he did not get her clothes off soon, he could hardly count on giving her what she so obviously wanted. His hands went up to the neck of her tunic, and clutched the fabric.

As they did, her eyes rolled toward him with an unmistakable assent in them. His grip tightened on the fabric, and he tore downward, with all his strength. The fabric was tough, but not tough enough to resist Blade's muscles. The tunic split open halfway down Mir-Kasa's back. As Blade let go, it slipped down off her shoulders and halfway down her arms. And as it slipped, her breasts sprang into view, free and fully exposed.

They were magnificent—there was no other word Blade could think of. There was no other word he could have thought of, even if he had been able to consider them and contemplate them unaroused and at his leisure. But he had no leisure, he was thoroughly aroused, and his merely contemplating any part of Mir-Kasa's body was the last thing in either of their minds.

Blade's hands followed his eyes downward in a single swift lunge, cupping the full ripe curves of both breasts. The nipples were already flushed with blood and hardened into solid little points. He felt them stiffen still further as his hands cupped and caressed and stroked. Mir-Kasa's head went back again, and her mouth opened to let out her breath in a great tearing, gasping sob.

It seemed that she was letting out all the breath in her body, and all her strength was going with it. She sagged down into Blade's arms so suddenly that he nearly let her fall. But he caught her in time, bending at the knees and bringing his lips down to meet hers. Another devouring kiss, and she was dragging him down on the floor, rolling back and forth so that the solid masses of her breasts swung gently to and fro.

Her head was back on the floor now, and her dark hair spreading out fan-like around it, making a dark frame for her passion-twisted face. She whimpered now, deep in her throat, like a wounded animal, and closed her fingers once again on Blade. He bit back a groan at the effort it took to control himself under the work of those superbly competent fingers. He sank to his knees, and reached down for her skirt. He reached down for it, reached up under it, ran his hands up bare legs on to bare thighs and on still higher. She wore nothing under the skirt, nothing at all. Blade's moving hands encountered a mat of curly hair already dripping like dewy grass with the queen's fierce arousal. As his fingers thrust and clutched and probed in and around that hair, Mir-Kasa's lips curled back from her teeth. Her passion was making her almost ugly, but it would have taken more than that now to repel Blade. Nothing short of a stunning blow on the head could have kept him away from the woman writhing on the floor before him. The woman, not the queen.

78

She had wanted to be treated as a woman, seen as a woman. As far as Blade was concerned, she would have her wish. And she would have one more experience as a woman instead of as a queen. He would take her as a woman, without deference or delicacy, responding to nothing except the urge in his groin and the pounding in his ears.

His fingers plucked and tore at the waistband of her skirt. It did not give way, but it was elastic. Inch by inch he dragged the skirt down. A stomach still flat as a board and showing only a few stretch marks came into view, with a surprisingly small navel set neatly in it. In a whimsical moment, Blade lowered his lips to that navel, and kissed it. Mir-Kasa paid no attention. He pulled the skirt farther down, exposing the beginnings of her pubic hair curly and dripping-damp as he had felt it, dark and shot here and there with gray as he had imagined it. Then suddenly the waistband gave way entirely. In a single jerk the skirt flew down over perfectly rounded and swelling hips. Blade flung it away with almost hysterical strength.

As he did so, Mir-Kasa heaved herself into a sitting position. A quick tear and a quick flick of the wrist, and the remains of her tunic went flying away to join the skirt. She sat before Blade, legs open, mouth open, eyes closed, now as bare as he was. Her arms rose blindly to thrust her hands into his as he knelt down in front of her. She hoisted herself higher up still, until she was half-standing. Kneeling on the rug there, with his arms locked around her middle, Blade took the Queen of the Tower of the Serpent.

She made neither sound nor motion nor gesture as his fearsomely stiff and swollen member burrowed its way up into her wetness. She was not tight at the moment he entered, but then her skilled pelvic muscles began to writhe and twist in a pattern as terribly skilled as the rhythm of her hands. This time Blade did groan out loud with the effort required not to release at once. But he only groaned. His effort to hold back succeeded.

Mir-Kasa beat him to their common goal. Suddenly her

eyes rolled up in her head and her arms locked around Blade like the tentacles of an octopus. Her body sagged down onto his, shaking and twisting and writhing as a whole series of massive spasms tore through her. Her body jolted and bumped against Blade, driving him down on to his back on the rug, with her on top of him. As they sank down, he drove still deeper into her, and her wetness poured down around him.

One small, lingering, rational part of his mind told him that he should hold on, keep going, try to satisfy her still more. But the rest of his mind was either no longer working or it was listening only to the uproar of his body. And that uproar finally rose beyond Blade's endurance. He arched his hips upward, and all his breath went out of him in the same moment that all his semen went out of him.

He went on pumping until it began to seem that all of his body's fluids were going to follow the semen. He had a moment's grotesque vision of his dehydrated corpse growing stiff beneath Queen Mir-Kasa. Then the vision passed. After a slightly longer time, so did his spasm.

He lay sprawled on the floor, completely drained both physically and mentally, barely aware of the pain in his abused shoulder. He was a little more aware of the Queen slumping down on top of him with a faint groan, letting his now limp member slide out of her. They lay there in a passive heap for a good while, practically bathing in each other's sweat.

By a heroic exertion of mind over matter, Blade was the first to recover. At least he was the first to speak a coherent word. "Mir-Kasa, I do not know about my own qualities. But yours are—" He could not quite find the proper adjectives.

He did not need to. Mir-Kasa dimpled almost like a girl, and her weary face broke in a faint smile. "Your qualities are—not lacking, Blade. Between your legs—well, that is a masterpiece that whoever fashioned you can be proud of."

She rolled off him and lay on her back, her breasts still

rising and falling with her quick breaths. She reached out and gently curled her fingers around "the masterpiece." Then she smiled again, and in a stronger voice said, "Are you wondering why I—took you—now? After your war and your wound and everything else?"

That was a question that seemed to require the same answer that Blade would have given anyway.

"Yes, I am."

"It was a—test. If you could do well—if you could show your qualities—when you were tired—"

"What marvels might I not perform when I was in really good condition?" Blade could not keep a slightly mocking tone out of his voice.

She raised a hand to his lips and gently stroked them. "Don't mock yourself. Your qualities are—well, Nris-Pol at his best has not done half this well. And he will not get the chance to see if he can do better. Tomorrow you shall become the Queen's Steward of the Tower of the Serpent."

Blade nodded. "What am I to do in that position—other than more of this?"

She laughed. "You are very definitely to go on doing this, and on, and on. And you will do it in that position and as many others as you and I together can think of. I hope that you have something between your ears half as good as what I've found between your legs. And I hope the first will guide the second. I love variety, and there has been little of that for me lately."

"I shall do my best," said Blade. And he added, with a grin, "Considering what inspiration I have, what else could I do?"

Again the quick dimpling, but this time it was followed by a more sober expression and tone of voice. "That is much of what you will do, but not the greatest part. It is what everybody will know you are doing. But the greatest part of what you will be doing, I hope none discover. That part will be more dangerous. But it will also have great results."

CHAPTER TEN

The first result of Blade's becoming Queen's Steward was that from a mere scoffing skeptic, Nris-Pol, the former steward, became Blade's open and active enemy.

Not that Blade really blamed the man. To sit in the Council of Wisdom and listen to the queen cast him down from the powerful office was bad enough. To see a man who had literally come from nowhere elevated not only to the status of a hero but to his old office was worse. And worst of all was sitting and listening to the queen's explanation of why this new arrival and new hero was receiving the appointment. Custom and good manners dictated that she veil the reasons slightly, but nobody had any doubts on the matter. Nris-Pol was being kicked out of the Stewardship and out of the Queen's bed because Blade-Liza was better at making love to the queen than he was. Nris-Pol was proud, and his temper became as foul as a half-starved bear's.

However, there was nothing he could do, except grumble and growl and spread evil gossip and ugly rumors. The stewardship was by law and custom and common sense entirely the gift of the Queen herself. "Common sense" was perhaps the strongest consideration, since one of the steward's duties was the sexual gratification of Her Splendor. With some queens this had been an easy job. With others, such as Mir-Kasa and her mother Bena-Kasa, it was a demanding job that wore out a good many of its holders. So

82

the queen's preferences would have ruled whether the law said so or not. Any Council of Wisdom that ignored the fact would have shown itself sadly lacking in the quality after which it was named.

The fact that Nris-Pol was as impotent officially as he had become in the queen's bed did not keep him silent. Nor did it keep him from causing trouble. A rumor that he spread industriously was that Blade and the queen were considering compensating the dead slave-girl's family for her administered death at the hands of the First Warrior. Blade found both the rumor and the idea that it could have any serious effect ludicrous. That is, he found them ludicrous until people began coming up to him and asking him quite seriously:

"Is the queen compensating that girl's family?"

"How are you ever going to find the right people? You must realize, the Low People breed like animals. They have no real families. They could never have them. So the money would never get to the people who deserved it, even if they did deserve it."

"It's a ridiculous precedent."

"It's dangerous nonsense."

And much more in the same vein. Blade started taking both the rumor and the talk it was causing more seriously, at least to the point of denying the rumor. Neither he nor the Queen were planning on compensating any Low Person for anything suffered at the hands of any High Person. Did they think he was a fool? Or Queen Mir-Kasa? Obviously a few people would have liked to say yes, but no one quite dared.

Eventually Blade mentioned the matter to the queen herself. The discussion that followed gave Blade a much clearer notion of how things were run in the Towers of Melnon. At least in the Tower of the Serpent, he corrected himself. Each tower had its own set of rulers with their own set of rules and rivalries. And the Tower of the Leopard was set apart from the others by even more than that. He still had not found out what those differences were, however, and he did not feel that Mir-Kasa was the right person to ask. At least not now.

But she was very eloquent on the problems of Low People versus High People in the Tower of the Serpent.

"Of course I wouldn't think of offering compensation. That girl was wantonly disobedient. She would never have fitted into my plans for the Low People." Blade resisted the temptation to ask what those plans were. He had already tried once, and Mir-Kasa had at once become exceedingly cold and formal. "It is not time for you to know them," she had said, with glacial politeness. "Please do not ask me again."

The queen shrugged and continued. "Besides, whoever said that the Low People breed like animals is quite right. It's all catch-as-catch-can down there on the Low Levels."

Blade ventured to inquire, "Are you sure it's their fault?"

Mir-Kasa looked at him as though his face had broken out with yellow and pink spots. "You sound too much like Bryg-Noz for your own good. Or my peace of mind. He was always saying that the Low People are wretched because we force them to live under wretched conditions, and nonsense like that. The present batch of Low People is useless. But in time—yes, in time—we shall see."

What was going to happen "in time" obviously concerned those secret plans of Mir-Kasa's. And it was obvious that whatever changes in the scheme of things in Melnon the Queen might be planning, doing anything for most of the Low People wasn't among them. At least "the present batch" of Low People. Mir-Kasa was not interested in reform or freedom or revolution. She would not have recognized any of these things if they had come up to her and bitten her on the ankle. She was interested in power—power for the Tower of the Serpent among the Towers of Melnon, power for herself in the Tower of the Serpent. That became even more obvious after Blade's next exchange with the queen.

"Why does everybody practically jump up and down and scream with fright or rage when they think of somebody helping the Low People?"

"Why shouldn't they? In all of the towers except the Leopard, the Low People outnumber the High at least five to one. Thanks to the War Wisdom the High People have only their swords and the Administering Wands. And there is one Wand for perhaps every ten of the High People. If the Low People ever got the notion we respected or feared them, they might begin wondering why they live as they do? They might even begin wondering how to get up to the High Levels and attack us there. And if they did that, we'd have to kill every one of them before they did the same to us."

"I see."

"Do you, Blade? Sometimes I wonder. No matter, if you do what I say, I care not what you think. Just keep your thoughts to yourself."

That was advice that Blade had been giving himself at periodic intervals ever since he arrived in this dimension. It was getting harder and harder for him to follow it. He decided to switch the subject, at least partly.

"Aren't all those Low People a terrible expense? I should think there would be cheaper ways of doing the few chores they seem to do."

His efforts to try arguing the matter logically were not very successful. Mir-Kasa snorted like a horse and made a rude noise in Blade's ear. "Once more, you're talking nonsense. What would we be, without the Low People to minister to us? And what else can a person win among us, except the right to have more Low People serve him?" She shrugged her bare shoulders. "The War Wisdom keeps our wars cheap and the Peace Wisdom keeps our wants few. If we had no Low People to order around, we might start making our wars bigger. We might start all dressing differently, or trying to furnish our chambers with many pieces of furniture, or eating bigger meals than our neighbor. We cannot live long that way."

Blade could not resist putting in, "We manage to live fairly well that way in England."

"Yes, and they have no Low People in England, to hear you tell it. Well, you don't need them. But we do. Without

85

the Low People, the Towers of Melnon would fall down into the dust and weeds of the Waste Land, and men would soon forget that Melnon ever stood upon the land."

Blade was beginning to feel that to fall and be forgotten was all that Melnon deserved. He was far from sure that anybody in any of the Seven Towers had anything worth bringing home, learning about, or even looking at. Their lives seemed to be a dreary round of stylized wars, petty politics and gossip, frugal meals (ninety different kinds of synthetics), and trying to dress distinctively when it was illegal to wear a color other than that of your Tower. It was a miracle that all the people of all seven towers had not long since died of sheer boredom.

Perhaps Queen Mir-Kasa was right. Perhaps the chance to order around, browbeat, torture, and kill the Low People who served them was all that kept the High People of the towers sane. Certainly Blade could see that working off their blood-lust on the Low People would make the warriors more willing to abide by the War Wisdom. If, when you felt really furious, you could borrow an administering wand and watch some Low People girl writhe in agony, you were less likely to run wild on the Plain of War. Blade sighed. The position of the Low People made the way Melnon was run more logical. It didn't make it any more appealing to him, though.

Blade did not find out for several weary weeks what Mir-Kasa's plans actually were. These weeks were not entirely disagreeable, for Mir-Kasa apparently could not get enough of his lovemaking. He could quite cheerfully have got enough of hers, however. Out of all possible bed partners, he would not have chosen a woman nearly as large as himself, whose appetites were insatiable and whose notions of loveplay sometimes resembled all-in wrestling. By the end of the second week, Blade had bruises in every place that Mir-Kasa could get a firm hold on him. Fortunately she did not mind being bruised in return, or Blade's head would have rolled many times over. He could not help wondering whether Mir-Kasa's psychological make-up was sadistic, masochistic, or an alternation between the two.

Apart from making love to the queen, there was little for Blade to do. His household duties as Steward were negligible; professional masters gave all the necessary orders to keep the domestic arrangements running smoothly. He did make one change, assigning a master of the First Rank to administer erring Low People, rather than following custom by doing it himself. He had to admit that he was not tough enough to watch people scream and writhe under the pulses of the wands—at least to himself. But he could hardly admit this to Mir-Kasa.

Instead he gave her a long line about notions of honor as a warrior that had been deeply ingrained into him in England. "It would be repugnant to my honor, my dignity, and my self-respect to wield the administering wand. It is not a warrior's weapon, for it is useless against a man or woman willing to either fight or flee. It is only an instrument for punishment"—he nearly said "torture"—"and execution of criminals. It can be nothing more."

"You think it can be nothing more, eh? Is that your objection to it?"

Feeling that Mir-Kasa was playing games with him, Blade nodded slowly.

She smiled. "Perhaps one day I can make you change your mind."

"I doubt it," said Blade stubbornly.

"You would," said Mir-Kasa. "You have very strong notions of what is right and wrong. Too strong, sometimes. But I think someday the wand will get around those notions, and you will find one in your hand." She gave him another cryptic smile, and drew his hands down to cup her breasts. Blade wondered what she might be getting at for several days, then he forgot the matter almost entirely.

Being a man of comparative leisure, he had a good deal of time to explore the tower, at least all the levels where the

High People normally went. He was particularly interested in the work chambers, where complex machines produced all the food, clothing, and other necessities apparently out of basic elements brought from God knows where. Blade was not sure that the current inhabitants of the towers could have created this advanced technology, but he had to admit that they were using it well. The workers, the lowest-ranking class among the High People, seemed to be the most sensible among them as well.

He also had time to keep his hand in as a warrior. He fought at least one practice bout a day against a good opponent. And although he fought in no wars, he did learn the fine art of using the lifters. In fact, he learned them so well that he occasionally struck poses while rising or descending, convincing Pen-Jerg among others that he did indeed have "a strong heart."

There were also the meetings of the Council of Wisdom, which Blade could not help feeling was rather ill-named. It consisted of the five high officials of the Tower—First Warrior, First Scribe, First Surgeon, First Worker, and First Master—and six women representing the rest of the High People. The six were elected anually. After seeing and hearing them, Blade could not help suspecting that they were elected largely for the number of their chins and the number of words they could get out without saying anything.

Not that anybody really needed to say anything in the Council. The work of the Council was by and large cut out for it by the War Wisdom and the Peace Wisdom. The only decisions that had to be made were whether a given action was or was not permitted by the relevant Wisdom. Nine times out of ten, it was not. Blade began to wonder if the concept of "crime" existed in the towers, apart from violations of the Wisdoms.

That kind of violation was comparatively rare, but it was punished with terrifying severity when it occurred. The case of a violation of the war wisdom arose during Blade's second meeting. A warrior was accused of having tried to get behind his opponent in the war fought the day before. The wretched man tried to defend himself, but was shouted down by the First Warrior with terrible curses. He was sentenced to be publicly stripped of armor and weapons, given ten minutes of Medium Administration (also in public), then degraded to the Low People for life. From the talk he heard after the prisoner had been hauled out, this was not a rare or unusually severe penalty.

That night he could not help raising a question with Queen Mir-Kasa. "Is it altogether wise, to send so many warriors and other able High People down among the Low People? After all, they do not lose their abilities simply by being degraded. It would seem to me that there is some danger of their someday getting together, finding a leader, and raising the Low People in that revolt you fear so much."

Mir-Kasa laughed harshly. "You do not understand how the minds of the High People work, Blade. To go down among the Low People kills their spirits and whatever abilities they may have possessed as High People. They are only shells of their former selves, perhaps *less* than the Low People who have lived down there all the days of their lives."

To Blade's trained ear, however, those words did not carry complete assurance. Mir-Kasa sounded as if she were addressing a public meeting rather than stating what she knew—or at least felt—to be true. He could not help wondering, and being silently suspicious.

His suspicions proved justified. One night a week later Mir-Kasa herself led Blade down into the low levels. And that night Blade finally learned the details of Mir-Kasa's plans—for Melnon, for her tower, and for the High People and the Low alike.

CHAPTER ELEVEN

Blade and Mir-Kasa were lying in the queen's great bed, amid tangled sheets and tumbled pillows. The queen lay sprawled on her back in a gloriously wanton pose, eyes glazed and dark hair spread out in a fan against the white sheets. Any stranger looking at her would have called her an absolutely satiated woman, beyond all thoughts of sex.

Blade knew better. He knew that those glazed eyes were deceptive. The real clues lay in the quivering red mouth and the long-fingered hands that plucked at the sheets—and occasionally wandered over to pluck at Blade's flaccid organ. He hoped it would not stay flaccid long. One of these days Mir-Kasa was going to demand of him more than he had it in him to give. That might easily be the end of his power in Melnon and perhaps even of his life. Certainly it would be the beginning of the end.

There was a peculiar five-beat knock on the door. Blade rolled out of bed, reaching under his pillow for the short sword he kept there. "Who goes there?" he called out sharply.

His voice awoke Mir-Kasa from her erotic daze. She sat up and shook her head, then made a placatory gesture with one hand. "Do not worry, Blade. It is the man sent by Bryg-Noz. Clothe yourself and bring me my black robe from the closet."

Blade did as he was ordered, but the name "Bryg-Noz"

started his mind churning. Bryg-Noz, the elder brother of Kir-Noz, sent down among the Low People some years before? It could hardly be a coincidence. But then what was a disgraced and degraded former warrior doing sending messengers to the queen herself? Blade had a feeling that the mysteries were getting more instead of less numerous.

When both he and Mir-Kasa were fully clothed, she signaled him to open the door. A Master of the Third Rank entered, bowing deeply.

"Blessings of the night upon Your Splendor," he said. "Bryg-Noz bids me say that all is in readiness."

"Good." Mir-Kasa went to a cabinet and drew out a broad green belt with two daggers on it. "Blade, arm yourself. We go to the lower levels now. I think most of your questions about my plans for Melnon will be answered there."

"I will follow where you lead," said Blade. It was a polite remark, carefully chosen to conceal his own excitement. Now perhaps he could start to make some sense of the mad ways in which the Towers of Melnon ran their affairs.

Following where Mir-Kasa led meant following her out of the bedchamber, out of the queen's chambers, and into the shaft of the queen. The car there was smaller than the one in the shaft of the warriors, and decorated in Mir-Kasa's favorite silver gray. But it dropped just as fast. Only a few minutes later they were at the level of the balcony, in the center of the network of corridors that ran out from the shafts to the doors that led on to the balcony itself.

Blade expected Mir-Kasa to lead the way down one of those corridors and out on the balcony. But instead she went only a few yards before turning into a side passage that led off into total darkness. Both the queen and the master seemed to know the way, but Blade could not fight back a moment's uneasiness. Could this be a trap for him?

Then he shook off the thought. Mir-Kasa would hardly have needed to roam about the tower in the middle of the night to get rid of him if she had so wished. No, she was telling the truth. Tonight he would find out her plans—or at

91

least as much of them as she chose to tell him. And perhaps a little more besides, since he was determined to keep his eyes open.

After perhaps fifty feet the master came to a stop, and walked over to the wall of the passage. Again that peculiar five-beat knock sounded. This time a section of the wall moved aside with a faint hiss. A dim greenish light flowed out of the opening. In the glow Blade could see a long flight of well-worn steps spiraling downward.

"Do not fear, Blade," said Mir-Kasa. "What I plan to do must be prepared altogether in secret." Blade nodded and followed the master and Mir-Kasa down the stairs.

He expected that the stairs would come to an end after about two hundred feet, when they reached the level of the Waste Land. But they did not. They kept on going, and Blade realized that they must descend deep into the foundations of the tower.

Very deep indeed, for it was at least another two hundred feet farther down before another door opened in front of the party. Again the master knocked, again a door slid open with a faint hiss. But this time a human figure was visible in the dimness beyond the doorway. As they stepped forward toward it, Blade saw that it must be Bryg-Noz.

The family resemblance to Kir-Noz was unmistakable. Bryg-Noz was two inches or so taller than his brother, though, and some pounds lighter. Good living was hard to come by among the High People in Melnon, let alone among the Low People. His hair showed more gray and his eyes showed more strain than his brother's but they might otherwise have been twins.

Bryg-Noz's voice was cool as he addressed the queen. Obviously he stood in no awe of her, for all his low station and ragged and soiled garments. "So this is the mighty stranger who bested my brother. Are his wits as fast as his swords?"

"You have my word for that, Bryg-Noz. You know well that I am a good chooser of men."

92

"Of men for one of the uses of men—yes. Of men who can think as well as please you—we shall see."

"You bandy words with me, Bryg-Noz," Mir-Kasa's voice held a note of gentle reproach. That was surprising. Had anyone else attempted to "bandy words" with her this way, Mir-Kasa would have flown into a screaming fury and had them punished memorably and painfully. But with Bryg-Noz she was almost gentle. Well, they had been lovers once. Some of the old bond must still link them.

Bryg-Noz shrugged. "I try to make sure you see clearly, Your Splendor. But I can only do so much. Now—is this man Blade-Liza to see tonight's test?"

"Yes. I suspect that he may be able to give good advice about using the Great Wands. His own people, the English, have strange ways of war. I believe they use such devices commonly."

Bryg-Noz looked inquiringly at Blade, who nodded. He could not have understood less of the conversation if it had been in Mongolian. But it seemed wiser to say yes when in doubt.

"Good," said Bryg-Noz. He turned his head away and called softly into the darkness. "Kun-Rala, prepare the testing."

"That I will do," came a clear female voice from the darkness. Then the master shut the stairway door behind all of them. In the next moment another pale green light glowed in the darkness.

Blade saw that they were standing on the hard earth floor of an immense vaulted chamber. As the glow lit up the walls and ceiling, he saw the chamber was two hundred feet wide and a hundred or more high. Its walls and ceiling were not the universal green. They were raw, rough, stonelike material, sullen gray even under the green light of the torch, and grimed and crusted with age. Down here in the depths of the Tower of the Serpent there was no need to color things green or keep them clean. Then Blade saw the people standing nearby.

There were five of them, four of them wearing the loose work tunics of the Low People and one, a girl, entirely nude. One of the Low People stepped forward and raised a hand in salute to Bryg-Noz and the queen.

"We are ready," he said.

But it was a she. It was a woman's voice, clear and cool. Blade could see the lift of breasts under the ragged and dirty green tunic—and the two short swords worn at a slender waist. A woman of the Low People, wearing swords and giving and receiving orders in the presence of the queen! Definitely the Peace Wisdom was not being followed here tonight!

One of the other Low People had a large sack slung over his shoulder. Now he lowered it to the ground and opened it. From it he took out a device somewhat like one of the administering wands. But this one was twice as long and twice as thick as the ones Blade had seen. It was silver gray instead of green, and around its butt end were a number of foot-long cylinders, like gigantic flashlight batteries. The man handed it to the girl Kun-Rala, who ran her fingers quickly over it, like an expert rifleman checking a newly issued weapon.

"Very well," she said, and turned to one of the other Low People. "Start the—the girl." Blade thought he detected a slight catch in Kun-Rala's voice as she said that.

One of the other Low People pulled out a standard wand and touched it to the naked girl. Only lightly, only briefly, and to the back of her knees rather than the back of her neck. So instead of screaming and falling to the ground to writhe in agony, she gave a little whimper. And then she turned and ran.

She ran out into the center of the huge chamber, toward the opposite wall. She went so fast that her white legs were nothing but a blur in the dim light. Blade wondered where she thought she could go. As far as he could see, there was no exit from this chamber except the stairs he had come down. And the girl was running straight away from those.

But she did not run much farther. She was perhaps a

94

hundred feet away and still moving when Kun-Rala snapped the great wand to her shoulder. One slim arm bent, and long fingers pulled back on a handle. There was a crack, a sizzling sound, the smell of ozone in the air—and the running girl simply flew apart. One moment she was there, an intact and entire human body. The next moment there was only a sort of bloody mist settling to the floor where she had been. Blade felt saliva welling up in his mouth. By a heroic effort he swallowed it, and turned an impassive face to Queen Mir-Kasa, who was looking inquisitively at him.

"Well, Blade? Have the English such as the great wands?"

"Not precisely such, Your Splendor. But we have things that can do as well." He was not going to admit that this—this *death ray* was far ahead of anything in England, or that the demonstration of it had nearly made him sick.

"Did you expect to find such as the great wand here in Melnon?"

He could not tell that lie with a straight face. "No, I did not."

"Well, they did not exist until a few seasons ago. They were the idea of a worker of the First Rank, a very good idea, wouldn't you say?"

"I would. But what are they for? I can see that they are an immense improvement over the regular wands, but surely you do not need these for—"

"For administering the Low People? Hardly, Blade. These are for use on warriors. The warriors of the other Towers of Melnon. And on the Low People, if necessary."

Swiftly, in clipped sentences, she told him of her real plans, and of how the great wands that could kill at a distance were the heart of them. She made the picture exceedingly clear to Blade—much too clear.

What she dreamed of doing was raising the Low People of the other towers in revolt against their High People. Perhaps they would not actually succeed. But they would shake and weaken the other towers so that they would be easy pickings for the warriors of the Tower of the Serpent.

"Armed with the great wands?" asked Blade.

95

"Perhaps. But I hope we will not need to use them elsewhere. They are for use mostly in my defense, and in the defense of the wise High People of Melnon."

The "wise High People of Melnon" were those who could or would follow her lead, and submit to her absolute rule. She expected there would be many, after she had made the Tower of the Serpent supreme in Melnon. But she could not be sure of all her High People even then. And certainly there would be many who would balk beforehand, if they knew of what she was planning. Raising revolt among the Low People was the most horrible of all violations of the Peace Wisdom, and the slightest rumor of it would raise a hornets' nest of opposition.

"And of course it is always possible that the Low People of my own tower may learn of what is going on, and try their own revolt. They would kill both the wise and the foolish High People, and leave the Tower of the Serpent too weak to support my rule over Melnon. So I must defend myself against the High People who would attack me, and against the Low People who would attack my friends among the High People. Therefore, the great wands."

The great wands, in short, would arm Mir-Kasa's private army, the instrument of her personal rule over both the Tower of the Serpent and the other towers. With them, such an army would be invincible and her rule unshakeable.

"No doubt of that," said Blade. At least no doubt he felt like expressing to Mir-Kasa.

But where to build up this private army, so that it would be all ready for the day it might be needed? Where in the Tower of the Serpent could the necessary secrecy be maintained?

The answer was obvious. In the levels of the Low People, the degraded and dishonorable brutes whose doings no one of the High People could properly care about. So when Bryg-Noz was degraded and sent down among the Low People—quite properly—he was sent down with instructions and advice from Mir-Kasa. He did not need very many of these, for he was a highly intelligent man. And each time one of the High People was degraded, if Mir-Kasa trusted him or her she told them of Bryg-Noz, and sent them to him. He used them well. By now he had—

"How many, Bryg-Noz?"

A look passed between Bryg-Noz and the warrior girl Kun-Rala. It was a look of complicity. Blade caught it. Mir-Kasa, fortunately, did not.

Bryg-Noz shrugged. "Oh, at last count, more than two hundred."

"Not badly done, my friend. But we need more."

"Of course we do," said Kun-Rala. "We know all about your thousand and more great wands in the secret compartments of the work chambers. But all it takes is one person with a loose tongue, and Nris-Pol or someone like him will have the tower howling about our ears. And you have as much to lose by that as we do. So don't urge us to move faster than is safe, I beg you."

The look Mir-Kasa shot at the girl was filled with chill rage. Blade hoped Kun-Rala would learn to control her tongue and her temper better than this if she was going to be involved in a revolution.

Then the queen took a deep breath and shrugged. "You are indeed the ones in danger, so it is just that I defer to your judgment. But remember—it will go hard with you if I find that you delay when there is no danger. Come, Blade. Have you seen enough for tonight?"

"I have, Your Splendor." He turned and followed the queen toward the stairs.

As they wound their way upward through the green dimness, Blade was turning the night's events over and over in his mind. Obviously his guess had been right—Queen Mir-Kasa was interested in upsetting the Melnonian applecart to increase her own power, not to help anybody. And she was playing a more dangerous game for much bigger stakes than he had ever realized.

But there were still some pieces missing from the puzzle.

Where were those Great Wands stored—and did he dare ask? And did Bryg-Noz and that hot-tempered Amazon Kun-Rala really see eye to eye with Mir-Kasa on the goal of the whole "revolution?" The looks he had seen passing between the two made him wonder. That was another point that needed exploring, before he took any active part in the affair.

Fortunately, it looked as though he would have plenty of time.

CHAPTER TWELVE

He did not.

In fact, he had only two days. That would not have been much time to find out anything new, even if he had been able to move freely around the Tower of the Serpent, and ask questions wherever he wanted to. In fact, he spent most of the two days in bed. At the end of the two days, he had finally brought Mir-Kasa to the point of satiation, exhaustion, and collapse, where she neither could nor would make any more demands on him. At least if his position in the Tower of the Serpent depended on his virility, it was safe.

But his position depended on a great deal more than that, as Mir-Kasa reminded him the morning of the third day. They had risen and were dressing in their best to attend the meeting of the Council of Wisdom. Mir-Kasa seemed more withdrawn and strained than usual, and Blade asked her if she were ill.

"Not in my body. At least," she added with a wicked grin, "not in those parts of my body that you have not tried to wear out these past two days. No, it is just that I am concerned about today's council meeting. It is an open meeting."

"How does that differ from a regular meeting?"

"As the name says. It is open to any member of the High People who wishes to sit on it and speak at it, about whatever may be in his mind. It gives the mass of the High People the notion that they have some influence. Usually it produces nothing except a mass of gossip and troublemaking. Fortunately they only come twice a year."

"Couldn't you postpone this one?"

Mir-Kasa shrugged her bare shoulders, making her breasts wiggle in a most interesting fashion. "Such a cure would be worse than the disease. It would warn all the High People of the Tower of the Serpent that there is something I wish to conceal. No, we try to survive this one, as best we can. Two seasons will go by before the next one. And before two seasons more have gone by . . ." Her eyes showed what she did not care to put into words.

They finished dressing. With the Queen's gray-clad Guards escorting them before and behind, they descended to the level of the council chamber. There was already a considerable crowd in the listening chamber outside, waiting to hear the council debates coming over the far-speakers on the walls. The list of those citizens who wished to speak to the council was already posted by the door to the council chamber. Blade and Mir-Kasa inspected it carefully, and neither could hold back a sigh of relief when they did not find Nris-Pol's name on it.

"That is good, but not perfect," said the queen. "He or someone of his party can still invoke the Law of Treason."

"How is that done?"

"One proclaims that one wishes to put a matter of treason against the Wisdoms before the council. That at once puts one on the speaking schedule ahead of anyone else. Of course, if one brings a false accusation under the Law, one is forever dropped from speaking at the Council."

"No doubt," said Blade. "But the council tends to panic at any matter of violating the Wisdoms. I do not imagine that there is much real inquiry into the justice of the charge, however mad it may be."

"You are quite right, Blade. Is that the way it is in England?"

"Sometimes," said Blade, thinking of witchhunts and the

like. "But I have traveled in many other lands besides England. I have often seen what people in power are likely to do, so not much surprises me—or escapes me." He hoped she might take the last words as a warning.

Mir-Kasa led the way into the council chamber and took her seat. Blade took his at her right hand. They waited—Blade trying not to yawn or twiddle his thumbs in boredom—while the rest of the council marched in with as much pomp and circumstance as they could manage. Many of them looked ridiculous, and Blade found himself now trying not to laugh out loud.

Eventually everybody ran out of ways of showing off and sat down, and the council actually got through the day's business. In fact, it seemed to Blade that some of the members were almost too concerned with getting through the agenda at a dead run. It was as if they were eager to get on to something else. Two of the women and the First Warrior seemed to be the most eager. Blade kept an eye on the First Warrior, trying to read the expression on the wrinkled face. Several times his eyes met the First Warrior's, and it was always the other man who dropped his gaze first. Blade did not like that at all. He decided to find a moment to warn Mir-Kasa.

But he did not get the chance before the day's agenda was completed. Mir-Kasa rose and intoned the formal words that declared the council open:

"Let all who have business before this open council come forward, in the order of their listing in the book of the council. Let their voices sound clear in the ears of the council. And let their words be heard and taken as wisdom for the better conduct of the Tower of the Serpent in accordance with the War Wisdom and the Peace Wisdom."

She sat down and turned to look at Blade. He met her gaze and reached out to squeeze her hand under the table.

As their fingers met, the sound of shouts and crowd murmurings burst into the room from the listening chamber outside. Blade stiffened, and he saw the First Warrior do the same. Unmistakably, there was a look of triumphant anticipation on the old man's face.

Before Blade could do anything more than say "Oh damn!" to himself, the door of the council chamber burst open. Nris-Pol strode through, dressed in flaming red armor from head to foot, and wearing not only his two regular swords, but an extra long sword slung over his back.

"He is going to invoke the Law of Treason," whispered Mir-Kasa. "The red armor is the traditional garb of a man who is going to make a capital accusation. It symbolizes his willingness to shed blood in defense of his tower—or of his accusation."

Blade nodded, but his mind was not on Mir-Kasa's explanations. Inch by inch he was shoving his chair back from the table. He wanted room to run or defend himself, just in case. And as he did this, he was also cautiously checking both his swords, to make sure that he could draw quickly—again, just in case. He didn't know how far Nris-Pol might want to push this matter.

Nris-Pol strode up to the council table and thrust out his right hand in its red glove, straight at Blade. He held that pose until he was certain that all eyes in the room were on him. Blade had to admit that Nris-Pol had a fine flair for the dramatic, whatever his other faults.

"Councilors!" shouted Nris-Pol, in a booming voice that could have been heard all over a room ten times the size of this one. Blade saw the First Warrior wince as the blast went off practically in his ear, and grinned.

"Councilors," Nris-Pol repeated, speaking now in a voice that was only normally loud. "I invoke the Law of Treason, that I may speak before this open council." He looked at Mir-Kasa, as if daring her to deny him the right to speak.

If the idea ever crossed her mind, she rejected it. After only a second's hesitation she nodded, then said formally:

"It is your right by your invocation of the Law of Treason to speak now before the open council." Her voice took on a slight edge as she continued. "And it is our right, the right of queen and council of Wisdom of the Tower of the Serpent, to punish you forthwith if you bring nothing of worth before us." She took another deep breath. "Say what you have to say, Nris-Pol, and be quick about it." That last sentence was not in the formal ritual, and Blade wished Mir-Kasa had not said it. If she was going to succeed in the revolution business, she needed more of a poker face. His own face was frozen into an immobile mask. He shifted his gaze from the First Warrior to Nris-Pol and back again, noting that neither could quite meet his eyes. Then he leaned back in his chair and crossed his arms on his chest. He crossed them low down, however—only a few inches above the hilts of his swords.

Nris-Pol launched straight into his accusation. "I bring a charge of treason against the Queen's Steward, the warrior of the First Rank Blade-Liza."

"What is the nature of my 'treason'?" said Blade. His voice was chill and remote.

"You seek to raise the Low People in rebellion against the—" began Nris-Pol. But the sentence was drowned out halfway through by exclamations and gasps of horror. They started as Blade had expected, with the First Warrior and his two women allies. But they were echoed from around the table, and from outside. In fact, there were howls of rage and bursts of cursing from the crowd in the listening chamber.

"Shut the far-speaker off!" snapped Mir-Kasa. "We can hear this charge without that pack of animals howling outside." Blade could see sweat breaking out on her forehead, and she licked her lips several times.

"Begging Your Splendor's pardon" said a woman—not one of Nris-Pol's allies "—but the law of the open councils is explicit. Those in the listening chamber have the right to hear what the council says, above all in an affair of treason."

"Very well," said Mir-Kasa irritably. "But we do not have to hear their howlings and screamings. This is the Council of Wisdom, not a collection of children who must tremble at their parents' voices!"

Nris-Pol had wit enough to take the opening Mir-Kasa offered him. "Yes, ignore the 'howls' of the people of the tower. Ignore them, ignore me—and then someday soon Blade-Liza's plans will ripen, and you will hear howls that you cannot ignore. They will be the howls of the Low People, rising against you, seeking your blood, seeking to set all the War Wisdom and the Peace Wisdom at naught."

Nris-Pol went on to describe in loving and obscene detail what would happen when the Low People rose against the High. He carefully avoided mentioning the details of how Blade was planning to bring about this rising and all its attendant horrors.

That was an intelligent move. It meant there were no specific points that Blade—or anybody else—could refute. There was only a growing mood of horror and disgust that Blade could now see on all the faces in the council chamber. Nobody would meet his eyes now, not even Mir-Kasa. It was as though he had suddenly broken out all over his body with some revoltingly unsightly disease. He remembered his own prediction about accusations of treason never being seriously and soberly debated. He wished he had not been so right.

The tumult in the council chamber and the listening chamber alike were rising higher and higher as Nris-Pol continued embroidering his accusation. An exploding bomb could hardly have been heard above the uproar, let alone a request to speak against the accusation. The expressions on some of the faces turned toward Blade were so savage that he checked his swords again. He wasn't sure that the howling mob outside the door wasn't going to break in and try to lynch him on the spot. If they did—well, there was going to be blood on the floor of the council chamber much sooner than even Nris-Pol was predicting. And not all of it was going to be Blade's or Mir-Kasa's.

He wished he knew what to do if there wasn't an obvious attempt to murder him in the council chamber itself. If he offered any sort of provocations, it would certainly set the mob outside into action. And under those circumstances, things might get so completely out of control that Mir-Kasa herself could die in the violence.

Blade shook his head. Whatever happened to him—short of a direct attack—he had to make sure the queen stayed alive and more or less in the saddle. It was no longer a question of maintaining his position and doing anything for the people of the Towers of Melnon. It was a question of the best way to stay alive until Lord Leighton's computer reached out from home dimension to seize his brain and twist his perceptions and snatch him back to England. So he kept his professional poker face on, as though it had been glued in place. Sitting upright in his chair, he contemplated the disorderly council and the now half-hysterical Nris-Pol like a king contemplating a mob of peasants at the gate of his palace.

Eventually Nris-Pol ran out of both things to say and the breath to say them. As his hysterical rabble-rousing died away, so did the hysteria of the rabble. Silence came down on both the council chamber and the listening chamber like a fog. Eyes swiveled toward Blade, and also toward Mir-Kasa. It was up to her now. Blade hoped devoutly that she would not stick her graceful neck out too far for his sake. That would be putting the pleasures of her bed before sensible planning for her revolution, as Bryg-Noz had feared. But Blade knew he could only hope. He did not dare say a word to Mir-Kasa. That would only make his enemies and hers more suspicious, more ferocious.

The silence dragged on, until Blade felt sure that his nerves were going to snap with audible *pings,* like overstressed wires. He took a deep breath and again fingered his swords.

Mir-Kasa's eyes met his briefly as she rose to her feet. Then they flicked away, and fell on Nris-Pol, who was kneeling before the council table, trying not very successfully to look humble.

"Nris-Pol, councilors," she said. Her voice was flat and

toneless, but Blade could detect the effort that amount of self-control was costing her. "A charge of treason of the vilest sort has been brought against my steward. I had thought him a virtuous man. Hold!" Her hand shot out, to still the rumble of protest that rolled around the room. "Perhaps he was once. But it is clear that he has wandered into evil ways." The faces around the table relaxed—except for Nris-Pol's. His face split in a triumphant grin. "Therefore he is no longer worthy to remain in his office, nor among the High People. By the Peace Wisdom it is given to me alone to pronounce sentence upon him."

She turned to Blade and her eyes again met his. "Blade-Liza, formerly Queen's Steward. I degrade you from among the High People. I declare that you shall be sent among the Low People, there to live or die as chance wills it. Never for all the remaining years of your life shall you again come among the High People. If so you do, your life shall be forfeit upon the instant." She raised her voice to a shout. "Queen's Guards! Come forward, and take Blade-Liza down among the Low People!"

CHAPTER THIRTEEN

Mir-Kasa's taking the initiative so quickly silenced the opposition for a moment. That was long enough for the guards to reach the council table. Their leader bowed low to the queen, then turned to Blade. "Come with us, traitor. Leave your weapons, which you are not fit to bear, with the First Warrior."

Blade rose to obey the order. But the mention of his name seemed to rouse the old man from his silence. "Your Splendor—" he began.

"Yes?" said Mir-Kasa coldly.

"It makes no sense—I cannot see—"

"What makes no sense and why cannot you see it?" said Mir-Kasa, an edge in her voice.

The First Warrior's mouth opened again, but this time no sound came out. Before anyone else could speak up against the angry Queen, the guards had surrounded Blade and were hustling him toward the door. As they passed Nris-Pol, Blade noticed the expression on the warrior's face. He looked as though the queen had just kicked him in the stomach. And Blade could see why. Sending him down among the Low People would put him out of Nris-Pol's reach. And he would be a major addition of strength to Bryg-Noz's "army." Nris-Pol obviously knew the first, Blade hoped he didn't know about the second.

The guards did not slow down below a trot until they were

through the listening chamber with its staring and muttering crowd and out into the corridor. They stopped for a moment to tie Blade's hands behind his back, then set off again even faster than before. Blade found it hard to keep his balance on the slick floors, and several times one of the guards had to keep him from falling on his face. It was obvious that the guards themselves were as much on edge as Blade, and he suspected that their reasons were much the same. They might not want to be involved in Mir-Kasa's conspiracy. But neither would they want to be involved in Blade's lynching. And that was a distinct possibility unless they got him down to the comparative safety of the Lower Levels as fast as possible.

All six of the guards let out audible sighs of relief when the door of the shaft of the warriors closed behind them and the car began its downward plunge. But all six immediately sprang to the alert when the door opened again. Two of them slipped out into the corridor and looked up and down it before signaling to the other four to lead Blade out. That made good sense to Blade. He didn't know how fast Nris-Pol was likely to recover from his surprise and start spraying orders by far-speaker to all his supporters in the tower. And he was certain to have supporters all over. The First Warrior and the two women were obviously in his pocket, but he would hardly have moved so far so fast without rank-and-file support as well. Blade hoped that Nris-Pol didn't have so many supporters that he would be tempted to launch a revolution of his own against Mir-Kasa.

By the time Blade had run through these thoughts, the two scouts had signaled that the corridor was clear. All six guards surrounded him again, and led him down the corridor to a recessed door. There they stopped, and again the leader turned and spoke to him.

"Here you leave the High People forever and enter among the Low People, Blade-Liza. Here you leave behind your name as one of the High People. Here you leave behind your honor as one of the High People. Here you leave behind your family as one of the High People." The chant went on for several minutes, listing all the things that Blade was leaving behind in passing through the door into the levels of the Low People. Then the leader stopped, cut Blade's bonds with his sword, and barked a one-word order.

"Strip!"

As all six guards had their hands on their short swords, Blade decided not to argue the point. He pulled off his helmet, and began undoing the fastenings of the armored tunic.

As he pulled it over his head, momentarily blinding himself, he heard one of the guards say, "What and who are—" Then he heard the sound of several sets of feet approaching rapidly—and the unmistakable rasp of swords being drawn. He struggled the rest of the way out of his armor with more haste than dignity. He was just in time to see five fully armed warriors come up to the guards and stop. All five had their swords drawn, and as Blade stared the six guards drew also.

The leader glared at the five. "What do you here, comrade? This is the queen's affair, not yours—or that of those you serve."

The five snorted contemptuously. One of them growled, "Nothing of the kind. This is the affair of all in the Tower of the Serpent who believe in the Peace Wisdom. This—creature—from the Beyond came to us, won the queen's favor, and now seeks to stir up the Low People. If the queen is so blinded that she cannot give proper judgment—"

"Watch your tongue, man," snapped the guard leader. He had dropped the "comrade," and his knuckles were white on his sword hilt.

"You watch yours, you shelterer of traitors," snarled the man who had spoken. "And what is he to you now anyway? We all heard you proclaim him degraded, by the Wisdoms." The other four men nodded. "Then by the Peace Wisdom he is naught but one of the Low People, and no law of the High People can have anything to say for him. And no warrior of the High People, either. Not even the queen herself, in fact."

The guard leader nodded reluctantly. Blade swore mentally. Once more he was going to get caught in the meshes of this damned people's wretched rule-mindedness. And it looked very much as if it might be the last time.

"Is this all true?" he asked the guard leader.

The guard leader did not condescend to speak to a Low Person. But he did nod again.

"Then stand back and let me have a fair chance at these louts," snapped Blade. "I can break any of them over my knee without even taking a deep breath."

The guard leader's mouth opened and he stared at Blade. "But you cannot—"

"Defend myself? I'll be damned if I'll just stand here and let Nris-Pol's gang cut me down like an administered slave girl." And before anybody could react to that remark, Blade moved.

His left hand rose and shot out, driving a clenched fist into the back of the guard leader's head. The man staggered. As he did, Blade's hands darted downward and snatched both swords from the falling man's belt. As the guard leader thudded to the floor, Blade glared around him and flourished both swords.

"Take your leader and get out of here," he growled to the queen's guards. "I've nothing against you. And you'd better go back to Mir-Kasa and tell her that Nris-Pol is sending gangs around to work against her royal justice. Get out of here, I said! I can take care of myself, and most of these floor sweepings too!"

He might have been degraded into a Low Person, but his tone was that of a man in command. And it was the tone that the guards heard—and obeyed. They snatched up the body of their leader and vanished down the corridor as if they were running from a forest fire. Blade took advantage of the surprise of his five opponents to set his back against the door. Then he flourished the swords again and grinned savagely.

"All right. Who wants to be the first to die? Or are none of you even worthy to wait on the Low People, let alone join them?"

The remark provoked a mad charge, as he had hoped it would. It was a charge much too frenzied to have any hope of success against a competent opponent. Blade was more than competent. It was no trouble at all for him to put his short sword into one man's throat and lop off the arm of a second. The scream from the second man echoed down the corridor like the blast of an explosion.

"Damn him," swore one of the surviving warriors. "He'll have the whole tower down here. You!" he snapped at the man on his right. "Run to a far-speaker, tell Nris-Pol we need help. Six warriors, at least. Run, I said!" The man was off like a shot from a gun, and the two remaining warriors turned to face Blade.

Blade licked his lips. "So Nris-Pol *is* your master. Not that I ever doubted it, of course. But Mir-Kasa may be interested in knowing this."

"She'll never know it from you," said one of the warriors grimly. "You'll not live that long."

"I wonder," said Blade. "Remember the war against the Eagles!" And he lunged forward.

If he had wanted to get away, he could have done so easily. But he knew that in the long run his only safety lay behind the door into the chambers of the Low People. His problem was to stay alive until the uproar brought somebody who could and would let him in. After that—but he would worry about that later.

Nris-Pol chose his warriors well, that was at once obvious. Both were first-class fighters, and Blade could not afford to take his eyes off either one. A continuous clang of swords echoed down the corridor. Blade also began to worry about attracting unwelcome visitors.

But when the response came, it came from behind the door. Blade heard it slide open with the familiar hiss. Footsteps sounded behind him, running hard, and he swung around and leaped to one side. Again he flattened himself against the wall, just as a slim figure in warrior's garb dashed out of the doorway, swords flashing.

The newcomer ignored Blade as if he were a part of the wall itself, and charged straight at Nris-Pol's two warriors. In an instant he was closely engaged with both of them. In the next instant it was obvious that he was badly outmatched. The leader's long sword came down with a terrific crash, and the newcomer's long sword sailed into the air and clattered on the floor. A moment later the other warrior closed, grabbed the newcomer's left arm, and twisted hard. The newcomer let out a high-pitched scream of pain and dropped his short sword as well.

But in their eagerness to defeat and disarm the newcomer, the two warriors had forgotten Blade. He reminded them of his existence by coming out from the wall in a lightning-quick lunge, with his long sword extended. Its point drove straight into the open mouth of the leader, smashing teeth, splitting tongue, and going on up into the brain. The warrior's eyes went blank, and he toppled to the floor so suddenly that he pulled the long sword out of Blade's grasp.

But the other warrior did not wait to take advantage of Blade's situation. Before his leader had hit the floor, he had released the newcomer with a yell of sheer terror. As Blade turned to face him, he turned also, and sprinted away down the corridor as hard as he could go.

Blade bent to help the newcomer, who was kneeling on the floor rubbing his bruised arm. "That was a damned foolish thing to do," Blade said sharply. "You didn't even try to coordinate your attack with me. If you had, neither of those louts would have escaped."

The newcomer nodded. "I know," and raised a wide-eyed face to Blade. Blade stared.

"Kun-Rala!"

Unmistakably, the face under the slightly askew warrior's helmet was that of the girl he had seen using the great wand the night of Mir-Kasa's "demonstration."

112

She nodded. Then she rose and grabbed his arm, almost dragging him toward the doorway into the area of the Low People. "Come with me, quickly. We have to get below, to Bryg-Noz!"

"How did you come to be here at all?"

"Please, we can't stay here. That one got away, and he'll warn everybody and—"

"It's your own damned fault that he got away," said Blade irritably. He didn't like being dragged about like a barge at the end of a towline without knowing why. He had put up with a good deal of it from his enemies, but he'd be damned if he'd put up with it from his friends—if they were his friends.

A moment later he wished he hadn't sounded so angry. Kun-Rala's face crumpled, and she burst into tears. Blade grimaced. He wished the girl would make up her mind whether she was a warrior or a woman. He didn't know how she was at being a woman, but so far she hadn't done very well as a warrior. He put his arms around her, and pulled her against his bare chest. The warmth and the pressure of his arms seemed to calm her. Her voice was steadier the next time she spoke.

"Please, Blade-Liza. I know I'm no good as a fighter. But Bryg-Noz didn't have many he could trust, to send up to watch for you. And I can lead you down to him. Let me do that, *please*. You must realize that. There's nothing left for you up here. And you can help us. You must help us."

Blade could not help wondering why he "must" do anything of the kind. But he decided this was the wrong time to ask any more questions. A moment later his decision was reinforced by the sound of feet and voices approaching down the corridor at a run.

Kun-Rala sprang out of his arms and slapped a section of the wall. She must have touched a hidden switch, for the door hissed shut behind them. The feet and voices stopped outside, and Blade could hear the faint pounding of angry fists on the door. Kun-Rala turned frightened eyes toward him.

"Please, Blade-Liza. Come with me down to Bryg-Noz. They may think you are so dangerous they will want to break through the door. And then they will kill us both."

Blade nodded. He hardly had any alternative to trusting her, other than going back outside and taking his chances with the warriors Nris-Pol had obviously massed outside. And it sounded as though there were a good dozen of them.

"All right, Kun-Rala, take me to Bryg-Noz."

CHAPTER FOURTEEN

They found Bryg-Noz far below, in a small chamber just off the large chamber where Blade had seen the great wands demonstrated. The general of Mir-Kasa's literally "underground" army rose to greet him, hand extended.

"Welcome to our ranks, Blade-Liza. Or am I being premature in welcoming you?" He made a quick gesture, and several men who had been lounging against the wall of the chamber stood up and drew their swords.

Blade laughed. "You obviously don't trust me much more than I trust you. I let Kun-Rala lead me down here because I would like to stay alive a little while longer. And up above that would hardly be possible. There were a dozen or so of Nris-Pol's henchmen pounding on the door behind us as we started down the stairs." A nod from Kun-Rala confirmed that statement.

Bryg-Noz stared at Blade for a moment, then shook his head wearily. Another gesture caused the men to put up their swords. The leader sighed. "Blade, perhaps you had better tell us what has happened today. Tell all of it, as it has appeared to you, and only what you have seen with your own eyes and heard with your own ears."

Blade did so. As the tale ran on, Bryg-Noz's face grew longer and longer, and he began pounding one fist into the palm of the other hand. Blade saw tears glisten in Kun-Rala's eyes and flow quietly down her cheeks. One of the men by the

115

wall was cursing quietly to himself. Finally Blade came to the end of his tale.

Bryg-Noz sighed again. "Quite a tale, Blade. Now"—and his voice was harsh—"tell me how you understand Queen Mir-Kasa's plans for—for the future of Melnon."

"You must have heard them often enough," said Blade.

"I have," said Bryg-Noz. "I certainly have. But I want to know how they sound to you. You may hear or see them differently from me."

"Suppose I do?" said Blade. He was even more tired of mystery-mongering and implied threats than he had been up above. "What will you do? If it involves violence, think twice before you do it." Again the men along the wall drew their swords, but this time Kun-Rala also drew hers. "Please, Bryg-Noz," she said. "Consider what he has been through today. You are behaving like Nris-Pol himself, with all your threats and growling like a hungry animal."

Bryg-Noz glared at the girl, but her words seemed to sink in. He sat down again and held his graying head in his hands for a moment. Then he raised infinitely weary dark eyes to Blade and said slowly, "Blade, I apologize. I—I am more tired than any man should be, who has to bear the load I do. If I could just get some sleep . . . But I must ask you again—tell me how Mir-Kasa's plans look to you."

Blade told him.

As Blade talked, he saw Bryg-Noz's eyes widen and some of the weariness leave them. Finally Bryg-Noz stood up again and began to pace back and forth, a broad grin on his face.

"I see. I see indeed. And you think that Mir-Kasa cares only for her own power, nothing for the Low People or for the future of Melnon as one people?"

"I think it sticks out like one of the Towers of Melnon themselves," said Blade flatly.

Bryg-Noz stepped forward and clapped both his hands to Blade's shoulders. "Then I think we understand each other. If you had thought Mir-Kasa really cared for anything else but her own future... Well, you said no more threats. So I will not make any. But I will ask you this. Would you care to join us and help us to make Melnon a city of free people, neither High nor Low, only of the Towers of Melnon? An end to the wars, an end to the War Wisdom, an end to the Peace Wisdom and our use of knowledge only to benefit a few?"

"That sounds like an ambitious program."

"It is. But what else can we do? Melnon today is frozen into a tight mold. If we can break the mold, and put something better in its place—"

"Can you put something better in its place?"

"We can try," said Bryg-Noz simply.

If Bryg-Noz had said anything else, Blade would still have joined the man's movement to "make Melnon a city of free people." But he would have joined it simply as a means of staying alive until he could get back to home dimension. Preferably with one of the great wands under his arm, but above all with a whole skin. That was as much as he could reasonably hope to bring back to home dimension from this dimension of rule-bound fanatics.

However, Bryg-Noz was an honest man. He had no illusions about his ability to sweep away all of Melnon's past and build its future single-handedly. But he was willing to try. And that kind of revolutionary rather appealed to Blade. Men like that did not operate on the principle of "kill everybody who's against you, and hope there will be enough left to build something bright, shiny, and new." If Bryg-Noz came to rule in Melnon, the Towers might be doing a good deal better than exchanging one bloody tyranny for another.

So Blade thrust out his hand to Bryg-Noz, and they shook hands until Blade wondered if his arm was going to fall off. Then Bryg-Noz sat down again and gave Blade the explanation the Englishman had been hoping for ever since Kun-Rala dragged him through the doorway.

Obviously Queen Mir-Kasa had no notion of what Bryg-Noz and the other leaders were planning to do with her private army. The revolutionaries were perfectly willing to go along with the queen up to a point—certainly they were willing to overthrow the rule of the High People in the other towers. This was bound to be a bloody mess, but was there any choice? But when the Tower of the Serpent ruled in Melnon, then the ruler of that tower would suddenly find herself—unemployed.

In pursuit of their own goals, Bryg-Noz and his comrades were recruiting among the real Low People, as well as the degraded High People sent down by Mir-Kasa. Instead of the two hundred they had mentioned to Mir-Kasa, they had well over four hundred reliable people and a list of sympathizers four times that strong.

That had been the plan up until today. But with Nris-Pol on the march, plans obviously had to be changed. If Nris-Pol had the kind of power Blade's story suggested he had, the "underground" days of safety among the Low People were about over. Nris-Pol could send spies to the low levels just as well as Queen Mir-Kasa. And when he had discovered what was going on, he could levy a charge of treason against Mir-Kasa herself. Blade had seen what that sort of charge could do. Mir-Kasa would be lucky to escape with her life, and Nris-Pol would rule in the Tower of the Serpent.

And then he would surely find the work chamber where the great wands were stored. What a man like Nris-Pol would do with hundreds of wands that could blast a warrior into red mist at a hundred feet or more was obvious. Tens of thousands of both High and Low People would die when he set out to conquer Melnon, whether he succeeded or not.

Obviously, therefore, the Tower of the Serpent could not shelter the movement much longer. They would have to pack up and flee.

"To the Tower of the Leopard?" asked Blade.

Bryg-Noz jumped up in astonishment. "How did you guess?"

Blade shrugged. "I keep my eyes open. They looked as if

they were trying very much to be different from the other towers. And I heard people talk. The Leopards, they say, worry less about High and Low People, and keeping both in their places."

"They do," said Bryg-Noz. "So they are the only people we can turn to."

"What are they going to think about becoming involved in a war against all the other Towers of Melnon?" asked Blade.

"When we show them the great wands, and tell them about Nris-Pol—well, I think they will at least listen. Whether we can convince them or not—that is another matter. But first we must get our people out of this tower, and over to the Tower of the Leopard."

That, as it turned out, would be relatively simple. There was a tunnel leading from one of the underground chambers to an entrance half a mile out in the Waste Land. It had been there since the tower was built, and had already been used several times by secret groups. Once out of the tunnel, there would be little trouble in making their way to the Tower of the Leopard. And then they would wait for morning, and ask the Leopards for entrance.

"What about taking some of the great wands?" asked Blade. "I think the Leopards would like a demonstration. And they might come in handy as weapons to use when we—return—to the Tower of the Serpent."

"So they might," said Bryg-Noz. "But Mir-Kasa allowed us only the one, and it has almost lost its power. She obviously did not trust us that much."

"Well," said Blade, "then somebody had best go up to the work chamber and take a few of the wands with us the night we leave the tower. Who knows where it is, to guide me? I am the newest member of your group, so there is nothing you need me for in the matter of leaving the tower. I am the most expendable. I know the High Levels fairly well, and I am probably the strongest warrior in the Tower of the Serpent if it comes to a fight. But I do not expect that it will come to a fight. I have done this sort of thing before, in England and during my travels, and I have much experience at it."

Bryg-Noz shrugged. "I believe you, Blade-Liza, and I accept your offer. But you will need a companion, to guard your back."

"Let me go with him, Bryg-Noz," said Kun-Rala. "He and I have fought together before. I can disguise myself as a warrior or a master and Blade can disguise himself as a servant that I am leading about. I can carry his weapons under my own clothes and he can wear a carrying frame to hold the wands."

"Very well," said Bryg-Noz. "You two have described your duties for the night of the escape. Now we must begin planning for what everyone else will do." He was not looking at Kun-Rala, so he did not notice the look in her eyes as she gazed at Blade. Blade did.

So he was not particularly surprised when she came that same night to the small, sparsely furnished chamber he had been given. He was drifting quietly off to sleep on the hard mattress on the floor when the door quietly opened and Kun-Rala slipped in. She stood looking down at him, as his eyes opened wide and he sat up facing her.

"What are you doing here?" he asked. He wasn't sure whether to be annoyed or amused.

"I don't know what I am doing here now either," she said with an impish grin. "But I know what I will be doing very soon." She was wearing one of the Low People's green tunics, a normally ugly and shapeless garment that she had belted in to show off her slender waist and young thrusting breasts. Blade could not help letting his eyes stray to those hinted-at breasts, and in return Kun-Rala's eyes drifted over Blade's body. He had thrown off the blankets that had covered him, and was sitting naked on his mattress.

Kun-Rala went over to the door and pulled it shut behind her. Then she came back over to the mattress and sat down at the foot. "I—I have not had much chance to be a woman, Blade. I have had to be a warrior for our cause for—for longer than I want to remember. I am proud of what skill I have as a warrior, even though I know it is not very much. But I want to learn to be a woman, Blade, and I think you can teach me well."

Blade could not help feeling the beginnings of arousal, but he could also not help wondering if this was the time and place. "Kun-Rala, why now? We—"

"Yes, we may die the night after tomorrow, Blade. We may die together, but that is not all I want us to do together. I want to learn from you more about how to be a woman before I die, if I am going to die that night." She shivered and held out both slim calloused hands. "Please, Blade-Liza."

Blade did not need to say "Yes," because his body was beginning to say it for him. And while Kun-Rala might want to know more about being a woman, she already knew enough to recognize a man's arousal when she saw it. She lay down on the mattress beside him, and her arms went around him. Blade could feel the lines of her body under the thin robe, and his own body said its "yes" even louder than before. She felt his stiffening maleness pressing up against her, and her lips curled in a smile.

He took that smile as a welcome, and his hands moved almost of their own accord to the belt of her tunic. It was a simple length of cord; his powerful fingers had it undone within seconds. Kun-Rala raised her hands over her head as Blade's hands crept down her thighs and under the hem of the tunic. Then they crept back up again, caressing the smoothly curved flesh underneath, raising the robe as they came. A quick jerk, and the robe was off and flung in the corner. Kun-Rala wore nothing underneath it, and the dim light in the room gave her body a weirdly beautiful sheen.

Now Blade's hands could roam freely all over that body, drawing small gasps from her as he touched sensitive areas. Her nipples were particularly responsive—dark delicate buds that sprang startlingly into solid life with a single brush of Blade's fingers. Kun-Rala gave a little choked "yes" as that happened, so Blade's fingers stayed on her nipples for a good long time, until she was gasping and writhing back and forth from that stimulus alone. At the same time her own hands were fumbling their way up and down Blade's body. Their touch was unsure and clumsy but delicate, and the unsureness, the sense that she was feeling her way, was in itself exciting to Blade. He felt a delicious ache growing in his groin, as Kun-Rala's hands crept down over the hard muscles of his stomach, to wrap themselves around him.

But he did not stop his own hands, for he sensed that Kun-Rala needed yet more preparation before she would be lost enough in an erotic fog for him to take her easily. He left off caressing her nipples and gently squeezed and released her small, high-standing breasts in an accelerating rhythm. She threw her head back, and her eyes closed. Blade's other hand could feel the growing wetness between her gracefully rounded thighs. His hand probed that wetness, and Kun-Rala's hips began to jerk from side to side, slowly at first but then faster and faster.

Eventually he saw and felt and heard that she was ready. He rolled over toward her, but as he did so, she rolled toward him, faster than he did. She swung up on top of him, he came up, she came down, and he entered her.

She was so aroused and hungry that her first spasm came almost in the moment of entry. She threw her head back and clawed with both hands at her close-cut hair as her pelvic muscles quivered convulsively and wetness poured from her down around Blade's thrusting organ. Her head went back so far that Blade had the vague fear that her neck would snap. Then she sagged forward, until her swollen nipples almost touched Blade's sweat-soaked chest. But he did not stop rising and falling, and neither did she. So she reached a second climax, and then when she reached her third Blade reached his along with her, and their bodies thrashed and their breaths hissed and moaned together.

She collapsed limply forward on to Blade's chest again, and this time she did not move for quite a while. Neither did he. Finally he found the breath to say, "Kun-Rala, *you* have been worrying about not knowing how to be a woman? *You*?" His tone of voice implied, "What an idiotic thing for you of all people to worry about!"

She wriggled happily, understanding his meaning, and her arms went around him again. For a moment he thought she was trying to arouse him again. But she was not. Curled against his chest, she drifted quietly off to sleep, and shortly afterward so did Blade.

CHAPTER FIFTEEN

Blade adjusted the straps of the carrying frame until they were as comfortable as he could reasonably expect. Fortunately he wasn't going to have to carry this frame or its load more than a few miles. Two hours' brisk walking even in the darkness should take both him and Kun-Rala to the base of the Tower of the Leopard. There the people that Bryg-Noz was leading out through the secret tunnel should be waiting. And, he hoped, so would a friendly reception committee from the Tower of the Leopard.

So far things had gone with almost perfect smoothness. Bryg-Noz was a sensible man; he had kept his plan simple. More than half of his people were to remain in the Tower of the Serpent, even more carefully hidden than before. They would be ready to go to work when the time came to take the tower. The most important two hundred would follow him out through the tunnel, to travel to the Tower of the Leopard, there to become the core of an "army of liberation." They would travel by night and should be long gone by dawn tomorrow. Blade and Kun-Rala would make their way to the work chamber in whose walls the great wands were hidden, and collect a dozen or so of them. After that they would ride lifters down to the ground and join the other party.

The plan was simple enough so that the number of things that could go wrong was merely large—not completely impossible. But there were still more dangers than Blade cared to think about. So he decided not to think about them, and turned to Kun-Rala.

"Ready?"

"Ready." She pulled her administering wand from its scabbard on her master's belt, composed her face into a scowl, and gestured toward the stairs. Blade composed his own face into the properly submissive expression of one of the Low People and shuffled toward the door. If he could just keep that expression, he was reasonably sure that no one would recognize him. His skin was smeared with dirt and grease, and his head was shaved entirely bald.

They climbed the secret stairway slowly, saving their wind and strength. Then they stepped out into the corridor, and headed for the Low People's shaft. Kun-Rala would have preferred to take the stairs the remaining four hundred feet up to the work chamber, but Blade had persuaded her otherwise. At this hour of the night there should be few people either High or Low moving about, except working parties like themselves. And the time and energy saved by using the shaft would be more than worth it, particularly if they had to fight. Blade hoped they wouldn't, but he couldn't be sure.

They had to cover about two hundred feet of open corridor from the head of the stairs to the entrance to the shaft. They passed one working party of four Low People being herded along by a candidate master, who bowed to Kun-Rala but said nothing. This was encouraging—at least mildly so.

There was no one in the shaft car that whisked them up to the work levels in the usual few seconds. And there was no one in the corridor outside the shaft door. But when they turned the bend in the corridor that led to the work chambers, they saw a guard standing before the main door to the chambers.

Blade swore mentally and drew Kun-Rala flat against the wall. There was thirty feet of well-lit open floor between them and the guard, and only a foot or so between the guard and what was obviously a newly-installed alarm signal

"This is new," said Kun-Rala. "The High People have never bothered putting guards in these areas before."

"Just be thankful there's only one," said Blade. "I think we can take him. If you will pull your robe down to the waist—"

Kun-Rala's eyes opened as she stared at him.

"Yes—strip to the waist. Then step out into the guard's view. He should keep his eyes on you for a few seconds. That will be all I need."

"You can't cross the whole floor before he sees you and gives the alarm, Blade."

"I'm not planning to," said Blade with a grin. He patted his short sword. "This throws fairly well." Then he patted Kun-Rala on her rear. "Hurry, now." She looked up at him with an expression that was not much short of worship, then undid the top of her robe and pulled it down until her breasts were bare. Slowly she stepped out into view, trying to give her body a sensuous sway. She was not very good at that, unfortunately.

But she was good enough. The guard's eyes widened as he saw her gliding toward him, and his mouth opened wide. Then Blade stepped out into the open, and his short sword flashed in the light. There was a meaty *chunk* as it split the guard's face open. His shout of surprise turned to a whimpering gurgle, and he collapsed to the floor, his eyes and mouth still open.

Without bothering to pull up her robe, Kun-Rala snatched a key from her belt pouch and opened the door to the work chambers. "Quick," she said. "Drop him down the disposal shaft. If we leave him here, somebody may come. And if they find him here they'll start their search in the work chambers." There was no strain or trembling in her voice or body now; she seemed entirely in control of herself.

Blade nodded and hoisted the body onto his shoulders. As he did so, footsteps sounded behind him. He dropped the body to the floor, snatching the short sword from its face as he did so, and turned to face his enemy. Then he stopped dead. It was his turn to stare wide-eyed and wide-mouthed, and behind him he heard Kun-Rala gasp. Pen-Jerg stood before them, both swords drawn and an inquisitive smile on his bearded face.

"Blade-Liza?" he said softly, though it was more of a statement than a question.

Blade momentarily toyed with the idea of playing the dumb and uncomprehending Low Person. But he rejected the idea in the next moment. It would be a waste of time, and dangerous too. Pen-Jerg appreciated honesty. Well, he would get it.

"Yes," said Blade shortly.

"You—are not supposed to be here," said Pen-Jerg mildly. "You could be administered for this, you know. And I suppose you killed the guard?"

Blade nodded. He noted that Pen-Jerg had said "could" be administered, not "will" be. Then he shot back a question of his own, in a mildly sarcastic tone, "What are you doing here at this hour of the night, Pen-Jerg, brave commander? Are you inspecting the guard posts for Nris-Pol?"

Pen-Jerg started as though Blade had stabbed him, and his face worked. Then he actually spat on the polished floor. "That is for Nris-Pol. No, I am making the rounds on my own. Nris-Pol has been spreading strange rumors of stranger things happening among the Low People. I wanted to see for myself whether Nris-Pol was spreading tales or not." He shook his head. "I am not sure what the answer is, now. What are you doing here, Blade?"

Blade told him, leaving out only the parts about raising the Low People in rebellion and about the great wands. He knew that Pen-Jerg would not stand for the first, and had best not know about the second. Not as long as he was going to be around Nris-Pol, who would probably have few scruples about torture.

When Blade had finished, Pen-Jerg stood in silence for such a long time that Blade began to get edgy. Suppose somebody else came along—somebody less sympathetic? Finally Pen-Jerg shook his head slowly. Blade braced himself, ready to try to jump Pen-Jerg and kill him quickly and silently. Pen-Jerg read the look in Blade's eyes, and smiled again.

"Be calm, Blade-Liza. If what you do is for Queen Mir-Kasa—with all her faults—and against the power of Nris-Pol, then I will not hinder you. In fact I will mount guard while you and your friend do your business in the work chambers. I think I will arouse less curiosity than that—" and he pointed to the body at Blade's feet.

Pen-Jerg hoisted the body on his own shoulders, while Blade and Kun-Rala darted into the work chambers. As they ran from room to room, Kun-Rala was looking nervously at Blade.

"Can we trust him?"

"Yes, as far as he knows what we're doing. He had no more love for Nris-Pol than we do. And in any case, do we have any choice?"

Kun-Rala had to admit that they didn't.

The particular chamber they were seeking was nearly a hundred feet in from the main door, and filled with strange-looking machines mounted on marble tables. Blade would have liked to spend more time looking them over, but time was one thing they didn't have. Pen-Jerg could be trusted for anything under his control, but some things would not and could not be under the warrior's control.

Kun-Rala darted to one of the machines, and turned it on. A low hum filled the room. Then she ducked under the table and Blade could see her hands going through the motions of twisting a combination lock. There was a faint click, and then the familiar hiss of a door opening. A tall cabinet in one corner and the section of wall behind it swung open, revealing a dark cavity. In the dim light Blade could see the sinister gleaming shapes of dozens of the great wands.

He joined Kun-Rala in the concealed chamber, scooping

up great wands and piling them in the bag attached to the carrying frame. When he had as heavy a load as he felt he could manage and still be able to run and fight easily, he turned to Kun-Rala.

"I've got about a dozen. Let's go."

"Wait," she said. She was kneeling on the floor by the racks, tying a bunch of the cylinders from the great wands together. Then she fastened a wire to one end of the bunch, and ran it across the floor to the door sill.

She stood up and brushed her hands off. "There. Anybody who steps on that wire or pulls it will set off the power tubes attached to it. And that will set off all the power tubes in all the great wands in the room."

Blade swallowed. "What will that do?"

"I don't know. Only the worker who invented them, and Queen Mir-Kasa herself, know for certain. It would probably kill everybody for several levels up and down. It might even blow the tower apart, but I don't think so. Certainly nobody will ever know what was in there, afterwards."

"What about the wands we're carrying, in case we're captured?"

"I'll carry one under my robe. If it looks like we're not going to get away, I'll set off its power tubes. There won't be enough left of any of us to put down the disposal shaft."

Blade swallowed again, then managed a grin. Kun-Rala might lack something as a lover, or as a swordswoman. But as a cool head in straight spy work, he had met few to equal her. He hoped she got out of this one safely. In a few more years a head like hers would be a valuable asset to the hoped-for new Melnon. He made sure the bag of wands was sealed tightly, then led the way out of the chambers.

Pen-Jerg was still waiting outside when Blade and Kun-Rala came out into the corridor, but the body was gone.

"Any trouble?" asked Blade.

"None that I couldn't handle," said the warrior cheerfully.

"Several people came by, but none of them knew that I wasn't the regular guard. But there will be trouble as soon as somebody finds the chamber door unguarded."

"Then we'd better hurry," said Blade. "Pen-Jerg, you lead the way. That way it will look like you're part of the escort."

With Pen-Jerg in the lead, they hurried back to the shafts. As they reached the master's shaft, the door hissed open, and four warriors in full gear strode out. Pen-Jerg fixed them with a cold stare.

"What are *you* doing wandering around at this hour?"

"We—I—" stammered one of the uards.

"If you can't explain why you're roaming the corridors at night like a cleaner from the Low People, I'll have to take your names."

One of the other warriors found his voice at this threat. "We are inspecting the special guards ordered by Nris-Pol. Here is our permission." He fumbled at the closure of his belt pouch.

"Never mind," said Pen-Jerg briskly. "Pass on to your duties." He led Blade and Kun-Rala into the shaft car, and the door hissed shut behind them. As it did, Pen-Jerg breathed a sigh of relief. "That was close. Now—pray to the Wisdoms, Blade, or whatever you English believe in. If they raise the alarm before we're out of this shaft..."

The car reached the balcony level before they heard a single sound from above. But just as they started out the door, a harsh rattling noise filled the car and the corridor both. The car door began to slide shut as Kun-Rala darted out, then it slammed shut on the trailing hem of her robe. Without losing step, she jerked the robe off and left it and her administering wand lying on the floor. Under it she wore her other belt with swords and the great wand, but nothing else except a pair of sandals. Neither Blade nor Pen-Jerg had the time or inclination to stare. Pen-Jerg turned toward the corridor to the balcony and broke into a pounding run, with Blade and Kun-Rala hard after him.

Blade was carrying more than sixty pounds on his back,

but the adrenalin pouring into his system gave wings to his legs. He kept up with Pen-Jerg all the way to the door to the balcony. As Kun-Rala darted up, the warrior flung the door open and motioned Blade and the girl through.

"The alarm's up," he said unnecessarily. "You know how to operate the lifters?"

Both nodded.

"Good. Get down into the Waste Land, and may the Wisdoms be with you."

"What about you?"

"I'll be all right," said Pen-Jerg. He drew both his swords and turned to face the corridor. "Now move!"

Blade and Kun-Rala both knew that Pen-Jerg was staying behind to face almost certain death, but both obeyed his final order. They dashed out on to the balcony and ran along it to the nearest cluster of lifters.

The lifters were normally operated by reel servants, mostly for reasons of pomp and ceremony—and also to degrade the Low People further. But the warriors of Melnon were not such utter idiots as to depend entirely on the reel servants. Each of the lifters was fitted with a full set of electronic controls that could be operated by the man on the lifter. In fact, once these controls were switched on, the reels above could no longer raise or lower the lifter. A handy feature for two people trying to escape from pursuers who sought their lives. But the lifter cords, tough as they were, could be cut. And Blade knew they would be cut if Nris-Pol's men got past Pen-Jerg.

As they reached the lifters, they heard the sound of feet running and voices raised in anger behind them. There was silence for a moment, in which Pen-Jerg's voice rose, high and angry. Blade could not make out the words, but he could not mistake the tone. And neither could he mistake the next sound—the clang of sword on sword. Pen-Jerg was starting his last fight, a fight for people who were determined to destroy the way of life the warrior had loved and served all his life.

131

There was no time to contemplate ironies, however. Blade's fingers flew over the controls of the lifter, setting them. Beside him Kun-Rala was doing the same, more clumsily. She had only learned the sequence from books.

But the clash of swords was still rising into the night when she finished. She stood beside Blade, staring down into the blackness below. There seemed to be nothing but night left in all the world, except the faint glows of the night-lights on the balconies of the other towers. Blade saw her shudder.

"Don't look down," he said quickly.

She nodded, a faint jerk of her head on stiff neck muscles.

"Ready?" he asked.

Again she nodded. He wound both hands firmly into the straps, braced both feet on the bottom bar, watched her do the same.

"Let's go." His thumb caressed the "lower away" switch, and with a faint hum the lifter began to slide down into the darkness.

As they passed below the edge of the balcony, the noise of the sword-fight rose to a crescendo. Blade wondered how many men had come against Pen-Jerg. It sounded like at least half a dozen. But the warrior was a good fighter. Perhaps he would beat them all off and make it to a lifter. Perhaps—

Blade's hopes died abruptly as a strong man's death-scream sounded in the darkness above them. It was followed by a thud and a scrabbling sound. Then a dim shape hurtled down past Blade, vanishing in a second into the darkness below. Another few seconds, and a faint thud floated up from below.

Blade had a momentary urge to send his dinner after Pen-Jerg. The warrior had chosen to hurl himself down to his death, rather than risk being nursed back to health and tortured by Nris-Pol. And Nris-Pol's men now roamed the balcony above without opposition. Did they have anything that could cut the lifter cords? Blade knew that an ordinary sword could not, but there were special cutting tools kept beside each lifter. How long would it take the men on the balcony to see the moving lifter reels, realize what was happening, and break out those tools? If they waited only another minute or two, he and Kun-Rala would be safe on the ground. Then they—

A bright orange flash in the darkness above. And suddenly Kun-Rala was no longer where she had been, a dim shape descending through the darkness beside him. Instead there was a white flicker below him—far below him—vanishing into the darkness. And another faint thud floating up from below.

Blade let out a yell of surprise and horror, and clutched the straps until his knuckles stood out white even in the darkness. He waited, expecting with every heartbeat and breath to suddenly plunge down after Kun-Rala. But the plunge did not come. Instead the cord kept running out, with its quiet whine, until suddenly his feet touched solid, stony ground.

Blade let go of the lifter at once, and the sudden loss of its support and the weight of his pack drove him to his knees. In that position, he finally did lose his dinner, and went on losing it for a long time.

When there was nothing more inside him, he rose to his feet and looked up. Dim figures were moving on the balcony, faintly silhouetted against the night-lights, and a distant buzz of voices floated down to Blade. He had to fight back a temptation to snatch one of the great wands from his pack, and hurl its deadly pulses upward at the balcony. But common sense overcame that first impulse. He stepped to the very base of the tower and flattened himself against the stone until the voices above died away.

Apparently Nris-Pol's men had not noticed that there were two lifters in use. And Blade's yell as he saw Kun-Rala fall had convinced the men who had cut her cord that they had finished off the only person escaping. It had saved Blade.

But it hadn't saved Kun-Rala, and Blade did not feel at all good about that. The girl would never have a chance to really learn to be a woman now. Nor would she ever be able to use her sharp wits to build a new Melnon. For the first time since he had arrived in this dimension, Blade felt a deep commitment to doing something about the rule of the Wisdom in Melnon. Two good people had died tonight helping to destroy it. Blade would like to see a few of the people like Nris-Pol die also.

CHAPTER SIXTEEN

It was just after dawn when Blade staggered up to the base of the Tower of the Leopard. He was staggering because he was carrying Kun-Rala's body in his arms, as well as the massive load of great wands on his back. Kun-Rala had been dead when he found her, her head twisted at an unnatural angle. But somehow he could not bring himself to leave her lying there where she fell. So he had picked her up and brought her with him.

Not far away he had also found Pen-Jerg, lying on his back in the middle of a patch of blood-soaked grass, his eyes staring sightlessly upward. The warrior must have been dead from his wounds even before he hit the ground. There was nothing at all to do for him. So Blade took a new, firmer grip on Kun-Rala, and staggered away into the darkness.

He was relieved to find that Bryg-Noz's entire band of two hundred had made the night's journey without trouble or detection. They were already sitting around on the grass on the outer side of the Tower of the Leopard. And he was further relieved to see lifters rising and descending steadily. The Tower of the Leopard was giving the refugees the friendly reception they had hoped for—at least for the moment.

Bryg-Noz was still on the ground, and hurried over to greet Blade. His face was grim as he stared down at Kun-Rala lying on the grass. Then he stripped off his own cloak

135

and covered her with it. After that he was all business as he quickly drew out of the exhausted Blade the story of the night's doings.

"You say that Nris-Pol seems to be much feared and hated?" he asked when Blade came to the part Pen-Jerg had played.

"I don't know any more than what Pen-Jerg told me," said Blade. "But he was a wise and honest man who kept his eyes open. I think we can believe what he said."

"Good," said Bryg-Noz. "Attacking a united Tower of the Serpent is not something the Leopards will care to try. But attacking one divided, hating its most influential warrior— that is another matter. I hope the Council of Leaders in this tower will hear us soon."

"The Council of Leaders?"

"They do not call it the Council of Wisdom, Blade. That is one of many things you will find different in the Tower of the Leopard. But do not question them too closely. They are a proud people, who will not take kindly to being told how things are in England. And we must give them no offense."

Blade nodded.

He had plenty of time to find "different things" in the Tower of the Leopard, because it was nearly a week before the Council of Leaders even heard the pleas of the refugees. During that week the refugees had nothing to do but eat large meals, take frequent baths, gossip with each other, and watch the life of the Tower of the Leopard go on around them.

It was impossible to call the Tower of the Leopard "democratic." Its people ran a variation of the normal system of Melnon, but with most of the silliness and brutality that had so disgusted Blade left out. There were certainly High People, who did all the responsible jobs, and there were certainly Low People, who did all the menial work. But a person from among the Low People could rise to be a warrior or a scribe or a surgeon among the High People, just as Pen-Jerg had said. And even those who remained Low

People did not have to put up with being administered to horrible deaths for minor violations of etiquette. They were expected to show polite deference to the High People, but they were not expected to grovel, and abusing one of the Low People was a serious crime. Blade could hardly say that he would enjoy living in the Tower of the Leopard. But he could at least say that living there would not drive him mad, the way living elsewhere in Melnon would.

The Tower of the Leopard was also much closer to a matriarchy than any of the other towers, from what Blade could see. The Council of Leaders consisted of ten women, who had to vote unanimously in crucial matters such as the war against the Tower of the Serpent. There was no queen. Instead the ten women who served on the council for life rotated the chairmanship among themselves for a year at a time. The First Warrior, First Surgeon, etc., existed, but did not sit at the council table except by invitation, and had no voting rights. On the other hand, the male officials had much more freedom to run their offices according to their best judgment. Nobody that Blade met in the Tower of the Leopard gave the War or the Peace Wisdom much more than lip service.

That, as Blade had suspected, was the reason behind the spruce and disciplined appearance that the tower's warriors made in public—and their deadly efficiency in fighting. The Tower of the Leopard knew that it was a minority of one among neighbors who hated it and its ways. Its sole salvation lay in making sure that it could fight as well as they could— or better. And it had succeeded. For at least the past five generations the other towers had agreed that there was nothing they could do about the Tower of the Leopard and its strange customs. Not, that is, without themselves throwing the War and Peace Wisdoms to the four winds. This was an even more appalling idea than letting the Tower of the Leopard strictly alone.

Understandably, the Council of Leaders took a dim view of an all-out war against another tower, particularly a war that would inevitably lead to a social revolution all over Melnon. Bryg-Noz made no effort to hide his planned final goal, in spite of Blade's advice that he conceal it. In fact, if it hadn't been for the great wands and the threat of Nris-Pol's getting his hands on them, the whole notion of aiding the Serpent revolution would have been turned down.

If Nris-Pol did try to get his hands on the great wands he would solve everybody's problems. And the solution would be heard and seen all over Melnon. But that was not Bryg-Noz's choice of solutions. He did not want to see his native tower smashed by Nris-Pol's mad ambitions. He wanted to smash Nris-Pol first. And so did Blade.

So they demonstrated the great wands. In Blade's now well-trained hands, one of them whiffed a couple of condemned criminals into the usual red mist. That opened a good many eyes among the Leopards. Bryg-Noz's descriptions of Nris-Pol and his ambitions opened a good many more. Within a couple of days, at least the warriors of the Leopards were enthusiastic advocates of war.

"In fact," said Blade to Bryg-Noz one evening, "I have the feeling there's more to their wanting war than meets the eye."

"How?"

"They tend to feel a little—well, downtrodden—being this much under the rule of women. I think they see this war as the best chance they'll ever have to get out and do something on their own."

"Perhaps. But their wanting war doesn't make any difference. The Council of Leaders has to give its unanimous consent, and so far they haven't even invited us to speak before them."

The long-awaited invitation came a few days later, but produced nothing. Bryg-Noz and Blade went before the Council of Leaders. They presented the same case they had already presented a dozen times before to the ten women, the youngest barely thirty, the oldest a wrinkled but sharp-witted crone who must have been well past a hundred. All ten listened politely, but the Principal Leader apparently spoke for all of them when she said:

"We will consider this idea. It is a great departure from all that has gone before. Though we do not bow to the War and Peace Wisdom here in the Tower of the Leopard, we do consider what will be good for our tower. And we cannot say at this moment whether what you ask will be good for it. Come again in time, ask again, and perhaps you will receive an answer."

Needless to say, Bryg-Noz flew into a towering rage—as soon as he was out of the council room. Blade spent a good deal of time in calming him down. Finally he got some wine into the Serpents' leader, and then some more wine, and then still more wine. Before too long Bryg-Noz was in a state where he would have praised the War and Peace Wisdoms if Blade had asked him to. Instead, Blade suggested that perhaps they didn't need to wait for the Council of Leaders to approve *everything*.

"I don't see why I can't sit down with some of their warriors and make plans, at least. After all, we're going to need completely new tactics and weapons to storm a defended tower. That's never been done before, has it?"

"N-n-no."

"I don't even know if they have what we'll be needing," Blade went on. "I can find that out in a few days, and tell you what I've learned."

"I—think—that's an excellent— *hic!*—idea." That was all the agreement Blade got before Bryg-Noz had to make a dash for the bathroom, but it was enough.

So Blade spent the next several days talking with the warriors and workers of the Tower of the Leopard, and inspecting their work chambers. He knew that preparing this war was going to be almost easy, compared with some of the jobs he had done in Dimension X. He did not have to train a corps of fighters almost from scratch, nor reinvent weapons lost for centuries, nor train warriors in their use. He did not even have to build most of what he needed. Practically all of it was already on the racks of the work chamber. Heavy metal stakes, mallets, lengths of the incredibly light and tough lifter cord, chemicals to make smoke—it was all there.

Blade would have liked to introduce the bow, but decided against it. To be sure, the lifter cord would make excellent bowstrings. But to make bows and arrows and then train any reasonable number of warriors to use them well would have taken a good deal of time. And time was what they did not have. Every morning when Blade went out on the balcony to gaze toward the Tower of the Serpent, he was a little more surprised not to find two-thirds of it missing.

However, there was plenty of time and plenty of material to make thousands of six-foot pikes. Each man in the attacking force would carry a bundle of a dozen or so on his back, and hand them out to the Low People of the Serpents. They would be used by completely untrained men and women, and they would give Nris-Pol one more thundering great headache. A man armed with one of them would not, of course, be equal to a warrior with a sword. But he could certainly keep anyone armed with an administering wand at arms' length.

While Blade was setting up the war, Bryg-Noz had not been idle in political matters. A week after the first council meeting, the two men got together again over more wine and compared notes. Bryg-Noz seemed happy again, as far as Blade could tell.

"We've almost done it, Blade. Eight out of ten of the leaders will vote for war and give us free call on the resources of the Leopards."

"What about the other two?"

"One is simply slow to make up her mind. Everybody says she'll vote for war when she does."

"She'd better hurry up. Nris-Pol isn't going to sit and wait forever."

"She will. The other eight are all pressing her to decide. It's the tenth one who's the problem. Ye-Jaza, the youngest one.

She's incredibly stubborn and short-tempered. Nobody dares try to influence her, for fear she'll vote against everything *they* want to try for the next twenty years."

"Is there anything to do about her?"

Bryg-Noz raised his eyebrows and looked at Blade. "Possibly. You are fairly—able—with women, are you not?"

The question so obviously had something to do with the matter at hand that Blade did not resent it. He nodded.

"They say that Ye-Jaza is—at thirty—a virgin. Now the tale goes that a woman is apt to be much influenced by the man who makes her a woman, if you follow my meaning."

Blade shrugged. "It is quite often just that—a tale. It depends on the man and the woman."

"Stop playing games, Blade!" Bryg-Noz took a deep breath. "Would you be willing to try seducing Ye-Jaza, and seeing if she will listen to you afterwards?"

Blade nodded. "I think the word is 'try,' however. If she's that stubborn and bad-tempered, perhaps that's why she's still a virgin. And suppose she takes it into her head to charge me with rape? That's a capital offense in the Tower of the Leopard, the way treason was in the Tower of the Serpent." Blade drew the edge of his hand across his throat.

"I know," said Bryg-Noz. There was a forced lightness in his voice as he added, "But didn't you once say you were the most expendable man we had?"

"I did," said Blade. He couldn't deny it. But he could wish he had had the sense to keep his mouth shut on that occasion.

CHAPTER SEVENTEEN

Blade had only seen Ye-Jaza once, at the meeting of the Council of Leaders. That brief glimpse had given him no clues as to her character. He remembered a small, slender woman, with a thin, almost bony face, and a mass of blue-black hair worn long like a young girl's. Not at all what Blade would call attractive, but definitely not ugly either. She had seemed to be staying remote and distant from the discussion. He suspected that she was a woman who knew her own mind much too well to be susceptible to any such simple-minded strategy as Bryg-Noz had proposed. But try as he might, Blade could not see that there was anything better they could do—at least without waiting indefinitely for Ye-Jaza to make up her own mind. They did not have time for that kind of waiting.

They did not have it, because Nris-Pol's position in the Tower of the Serpent was growing stronger each day. About every third day the underground group remaining in the tower sent over a messenger, and the messages always told the same story. Nris-Pol was strengthening the guards, and assigning to them warriors loyal to himself. Nris-Pol had caused seven prominent warriors who opposed him to be degraded to the Low People on false charges of treason and violations of the Wisdoms. Nris-Pol had caused four women who spoke against him to be sent to the pleasure chambers. Nris-Pol had done this, Nris-Pol had done that, Nris-Pol, Nris-Pol—always Nris-Pol.

One day Blade exploded in frustrated fury, "What the devil is Queen Mir-Kasa doing about all this? Can't she do anything against Nris-Pol?"

"She can keep herself alive," said Bryg-Noz shortly. The strain was telling on him even more than it was on Blade. The lines in his face were growing deeper each day, and even his hair seemed to be growing grayer. "And that is about all she can really do. Unless—"

"Yes?"

"Unless she guesses what we are planning and what Nris-Pol is planning. She might—she's no fool. And if she does, she might be waiting for us to attack, so that we and Nris-Pol can destroy each other."

Blade nodded. "Leaving her in complete command of the Tower of the Serpent—or what's left of it." He shrugged. "If she knew what we were really planning, that would be very short-sighted of her. But I don't suppose she knows about our plans for raising the Low People."

"I hope not," said Bryg-Noz grimly. And there they had to leave the matter.

Fortunately, good news came before Bryg-Noz's hair had turned entirely white. Ye-Jaza invited Blade to a private dinner in her chambers.

"Marvelous!" said Bryg-Noz. "You can begin making an impression on her now. But for the Wisdoms, don't move too fast!"

"Didn't you say I had a way with women?" said Blade sourly. "Then leave this to my judgment." Reluctantly, Bryg-Noz agreed.

In fact, there was no opportunity to move fast or slowly at that dinner. It was "private" only in the sense that there were no more than a dozen people there. They seemed to be there principally to provide an audience for Ye-Jaza, however. If she had been silent and remote in the council meeting, she was certainly not that way at the dinner. Her mouth hardly ever closed, except to chew her food, for the space of two whole hours. This might have been deadly dull, except that she at least had a well-stocked, even brilliant mind. Her conversation would have been fascinating if there hadn't been so bloody much of it! There was no opening all evening for Blade to do anything but sit back and be part of the passive audience for the autocratic hostess.

Bryg-Noz, who had let his hopes rise unreasonably high, was greatly downcast by Blade's report.

"Isn't there anything you could have done?" he implored.

"Certainly," snapped Blade. "I could have snatched Ye-Jaza from her chair and raped her on her own dining table in front of her own guests in the middle of her own tableware. But that wouldn't have done us any good. There was nothing I could have done that would have helped us."

Bryg-Noz glowered at Blade, but kept his peace. At least he had enough sense to let "the one who fights the bull" do the job the way he saw it.

In any case, four days later Blade got another invitation to one of Ye-Jaza's parties. There were only six people this time, and Blade found at least one of the openings he had been looking for. Something Ye-Jaza said reminded Blade of something he had encountered on his own travels elsewhere in Dimension X. Breaking into a pause in Ye-Jaza's flow of words, he began telling anecdotes of those travels. He had always been a reasonably good conversationalist, but now he knew he had to rise to unusual heights.

He succeeded. Before Ye-Jaza had her mouth empty and was ready to start talking again, Blade had the other four at the table listening entirely to him. And this time it was to him that they listened for the remaining two hours of the dinner party. The four were obviously fascinated. Ye-Jaza glowered for a few minutes—being shut out of the conversation at her own dinner table was something new for her. Then she stopped glowering and started listening. Gradually her expression changed, and began to show interest, then fascination, then finally even a little awe. When the party finally broke up—hours after it was supposed to—Ye-Jaza's

144

eyes followed Blade out the door with unmistakable interest.

This was all very well as far as it went, but that was not very far. Fortunately there was no more bad news from the Tower of the Serpent for several days. Nris-Pol had apparently done as much consolidating of his position as he thought he needed to, at least for the moment.

Then on the fifth day two things happened. Blade received another invitation from Ye-Jaza, this one sent by messenger and written on perfumed paper. And word came from the Tower of the Serpent that Queen Mir-Kasa had appointed Bryg-Noz's younger brother Kir-Noz to be Queen's Steward. Bryg-Noz was in a sweat of anxiety over this, although he could not really say whether it was good news or bad news.

"A little of both," he finally said with a sigh. "If Mir-Kasa can appoint somebody with so little love for Nris-Pol, she must not yet be completely helpless. And Kir-Noz will be a good man to have giving orders to her guards and standing between her and the ambitions of Nris-Pol.

"But that also makes him Nris-Pol's first target, doesn't it?" said Blade.

Bryg-Noz nodded wearily. "Yes. Nris-Pol's next move will be my brother's death sentence. It cannot be otherwise. Before Nris-Pol is ready to move, we must be." Bryg-Noz did not add any urgings to Blade this time. He knew that Blade was moving as fast as he could.

Blade nearly moved all the way to his goal that same night. When he arrived in Ye-Jaza's dining chamber, he saw that the table was laid out for only two people. And a large bottle of what both looked and smelled like wine stood in the middle of the table.

Ye-Jaza appeared a moment later. When she did, Blade wondered who was planning to seduce whom. She wore a gown of shimmering black and green threads that flowed around her slender limbs. As far as Blade could see, she wore nothing at all under it. Her hair was piled high on top of her small head, and a thin gold circlet shone against the blackness of the hair. She seemed slightly ill at ease, and there was a definitely strained note in her voice as she welcomed Blade and told him to sit down.

The meal came on, course after course, spicier than usual. This inevitably produced a lively thirst, and that was where the wine bottle came in. Blade saw that Ye-Jaza was drinking twice as much as usual. He held himself back, carefully not keeping pace with her.

Gradually Ye-Jaza's eyes began to sparkle as they had never done before, her movements became quick and lively, and her laughter louder and more prolonged. Her speech did not become slurred, but it flowed less readily. For the first time the conversation actually flowed back and forth between the two of them, instead of being a monologue by one or the other.

Blade became more and more aware of Ye-Jaza's real physical attractiveness as the meal wore on. And he became less and less able to keep his eyes off her. It was particularly hard to do this when she leaned back in her chair, and the outlines of small but well-formed breasts appeared under her gown. There was definitely nothing else covering them except that gown.

Dessert came, and with it a second bottle of wine. Ye-Jaza's laughter now occasionally faded out in a girlish giggle. Her dignity had almost entirely fallen away. Or had she perhaps let it drop deliberately?

But nothing further happened, and he decided it was best not to make anything happen this time—unless Ye-Jaza asked for it. He rose to leave, taking great care where he put his feet. He weighed nearly twice as much as the woman, and had drunk barely half as much wine. But it had been strong wine.

Ye-Jaza rose also, tottering slightly on her high heels, and keeping her face straight with obvious difficulty. She came around the table toward Blade, coming closer and closer until she was just one step beyond the reach of his arms. Blade stood motionless, waiting for her to take that last step of her own free will.

She took it, and slowly his arms closed around her, pulling her gently the rest of the way against him. He saw her slim white throat contract several times as she swallowed rapidly. Suddenly there was a glaze of sweat on her high forehead. Blade's hands ran down to the small of her back, fingers playing a gentle rhythm along her spine. Then they rose and stroked the sides of her neck, from just below the small neat ears down to the shoulders of her gown. Definitely she had nothing on under the gown. Blade could feel the warmth of her body striking through the threads, and soft round limbs pressing harder and harder against his. Genuine desire was in him as he moved his hands down lower, over the gentle upper curves of her breasts.

Her throat contracted again, and this time her breasts rose also as she took in a deep breath. "N-n-no," she said. It seemed to Blade that she was talking more to her own body, denying its urgings, than she was to him. She took another deep breath. "I—you don't—not—this—" Between the wine and the arousal she could barely talk coherently.

She did not back out of Blade's arms. Instead he let his hands fall away, and stepped back, looking straight into her eyes as he did so. They seemed larger than ever before, and they were filled with tears. "I'll be back," he said softly, as he turned to go.

Outside Blade took a deep breath of his own, and let it out in a sigh of relief. The physical attraction was there, and so were the responses of Ye-Jaza's unawakened body. But she still had to decide whether to let that body wake fully, or try to club it back into its sleep. He wondered how long it would take her to decide.

Bryg-Noz was waiting in their chambers when Blade returned. He was obviously as excited as a schoolboy about something. But he could not help noticing the expression on Blade's face.

"Did you—?"

Blade held thumb and forefinger about half an inch apart. "This close."

"Do you think you can do it the next time?"

"How the devil should I know?" exploded Blade. "Women are unpredictable creatures at best. Those who are still virgins at thirty are more so than most. Besides, what makes you think that simply one night with me will make Ye-Jaza my slave? It may take weeks even after I reach my first goal, damn it!"

Bryg-Noz sighed. "I know, Blade. In my head I know all of these things, but in my heart—" He shrugged. "There is important news from the Tower of the Serpent. Nris-Pol has organized a war with the Tower of the Ox. He is sending out one hundred warriors."

Blade's lips pursed in a silent whistle. That was by far the largest war party he had ever heard about. The usual war party was the forty he had seen his first day in Melnon; occasionally there were fifty or sixty. But a hundred?

"Who are they?" he asked, his voice sharp.

Bryg-Noz looked bewildered. "What do you mean?"

"I mean—are they all of Nris-Pol's own faction, or are they his enemies, or is it a mixture, or what? That makes a difference—an enormous difference."

"Yes, I can see that it would." Bryg-Noz might be confused briefly, but he never stayed that way for long. "As far as I know, Nris-Pol is sending out only warriors who are not of his faction."

Blade nodded. "That is not good. It suggests to me that he wants to get the hard core of the opposition out of the Tower of the Serpent and involved in fighting a war. That would leave him free to make some dramatic move—against Mir-Kasa, for example."

"Or breaking out the great wands," said Bryg-Noz grimly.

"Exactly," said Blade. "When is the war going to be fought?"

"The second day of the next ten-day."

Blade grimaced. That was only seven days away. Seven days was hardly enough time for getting everything ready, even if they started now. And they couldn't start now. But equally well they couldn't just sit and wait.

Blade grimaced again and slapped Bryg-Noz on the shoulder. "My friend, you know what the plans for the war—the real war—are. So does the First Warrior here. You and he should get together at once, and start picking men for key positions. Plan on our striking the day of the war against the Tower of the Ox. With a hundred Serpent warriors out of the way, our job will be easier."

"But—" began Bryg-Noz, and then he closed his mouth with a decisive snap of teeth. "Very well. But if the First Warrior is detected—"

"I know. It will mean his position. But he will not be detected. At least not by the only leader we have to fear, Ye-Jaza. I'll be keeping her too busy!"

"You'll be keeping her too busy," Bryg-Noz echoed. He shook his head. "You seem to be very confident all of a sudden."

"I am—somewhat," said Blade. "But even if I weren't—do we want to run any avoidable risk of finding the balcony of the Tower of the Serpent lined with Nris-Pol's men, all carrying great wands?"

There was no answer to that question, so Blade and Bryg-Noz shook hands on their agreement and settled down to planning. Blade also sent off a message to Ye-Jaza, inviting *her* to dine privately in *his* chambers. It was a bold reversal of the female-dominated etiquette of the Tower of the Leopard. But Blade knew that if Ye-Jaza accepted, he was one more long step toward his goal.

She did. Blade forgot about planning for the war in a flurry of planning for the dinner. Food, drink, decorations, his own clothing (shorts and boots only)—he chose them all with an eye to creating the most relaxed and erotic atmosphere he could imagine.

He set the dinner for the very next evening. The fact that Ye-Jaza accepted on such short notice suggested that she was already half-willing to do his bidding. But only in minor matters, and the war was not a minor matter. Blade did not like having the whole future of a dimension depend on his skill as a host and a seducer, but there seemed to be no way out of the situation.

So he was relaxed and calm as he greeted Ye-Jaza and smiled down at her. She was easy to smile at tonight. Her gown was the same mass of threads with nothing underneath, but this time the colors were red and black. And the circlet in her high-piled hair was silver instead of gold. Her shoes were high-heeled, also black and red. She was not quite shaking in those shoes as she held out her hand to Blade, but he could see and feel the tension in her.

Her eyes never left his face as the servants brought in the food and the jug of wine. Her tongue kept creeping out between her small even white teeth and creeping back again. She gulped one, two, three glasses of the wine without doing more than pecking at her food. She was obviously doing it deliberately, and Blade knew that *she* knew what was in his mind. The only question was—what did she think of it?

She settled that matter almost in the next moment. Putting her glass down with a solid thump on the table, she fixed Blade with a stare and a grim little smile. "I know what you want, Blade-Liza. I do not know whether I want it. But I want to decide with a clear head. I will take no more wine. But you will come here, Blade-Liza, and you will *try* to take me."

That was not the warmest invitation that Blade had ever received from a woman. But his heart leaped within him at her words. Here was his chance. Now to make the best of it.

They both rose in the same moment, and stepped away from the table. Blade raised his arms, and once more Ye-Jaza moved into them, step by step. But this time her own arms were raised as well. As his went around her, so did hers go around him. She clung to him with surprising strength, but Blade could feel her trembling. She was clinging to him for support rather than in passion.

He ran his hands up and down her back, and this time he did slip his fingers in through the threads. His fingers touched bare skin, smooth and warm and firm. He heard a little gasp. His hands moved down, until they were at the small of her back. They moved farther still, until he felt the swell of her buttocks. The gasp came again, louder. Her arms tightened still more, and Blade felt the small "give" as her breasts pressed against him. Unmistakably, he could feel the hardening buds of rising nipples through the threads.

He bent down and began kissing her, moving his lips slowly from place to place. Forehead—a chaste kiss such as a brother might have given—then both eyes, the tip of her rather prominent nose, both cheeks, ears, the sides of her neck—and finally full on the lips.

Those lips were dry and tight under his for a moment, a second moment, a third. Then they opened, slowly at first, then in a rush into great warm clinging wet blossoms that seemed to want to suck him in. Her tongue came out and caressed his. He saw her eyes roll up and close, and for a moment he thought she was going to faint. Her body stiffened and her breathing slowed almost to the vanishing point. For what seemed like an age she stood like that against him. Then her hands moved, and they did not push him away. Instead they closed on his hands and drew them around from her back to her stomach, Then her slim fingers released his to push the threads aside from her breasts and let his hands in.

They were the breasts of a girl rather than of a woman, in size but also in firmness. Blade's hands each cupped one very nicely, and he felt the surprisingly large nipples harden still further against his palms. Vaguely he wondered what color they would be.

Now her hands were moving again, across his shoulders and down his back, to tighten around him and pull him still more tightly against her. And in that moment Blade knew that he was through her last barrier. Ye-Jaza was listening now only to the call of her body, a body waiting and ready to be transformed in all ways into a woman's.

Blade heard the call of his own body too, and so he picked her up in his arms, his lips caressing her throat as he did so.

She was even lighter in his arms than he had expected. It was no effort at all to carry her to the bedchamber. He lowered her on to the bed, then turned aside to take off his shorts and boots.

He was half-afraid this necessary pause might give her a chance to change her mind, but she did not. When he turned back to her, naked, his arousal jutting out before him like a ship's bowsprit, she was lying where he had left her. Her eyes turned toward him, and widened as they took in his erection. But there was no fear or flinching in those eyes. Ye-Jaza seemed to have retreated into some private world of her own, beyond resisting him—but perhaps beyond feeling him or responding to him also. He would have to follow her into that private world, in order to get the results he wanted.

He lay down on the bed beside her. His hands could roam freely all over her body, and they did so. He spent a long time on her breasts, and before that time passed those breasts were rising and falling with the frantic speed of her breathing. Then his hands darted swiftly down over the flat stomach, to burrow between her thighs. Those thighs spread apart slowly but surely as his hands reached the crucial point, and a long slow shudder racked her body. Not a climax—not yet. Just the reaction to new and uncontrollable sensations, beyond what her mind had conceived or her body had felt until now.

The hair between Ye-Jaza's thighs was a small mat of silky strands, already beginning to go limp with the wetness of her arousal. But Blade did not take that first wetness as his cue to enter. Instead he let his fingers work up and down her body again, both on the front and the back, gradually peeling away the threads of the gown until she was as naked as he was. Once her eyes flickered down at her bare body, widening in surprise. But she did not stiffen or stop or speak. Instead she shook her head and gave a little whimper that might have been delight, might have been protest. Her pubic hair was so black it was almost blue, Blade noted. And those now outrageously swollen nipples were solid cones of chocolate brown.

Eventually Blade noticed that her gasps and moans were coming almost continuously, and her eyes were riveted on his erection. It was as if she wanted to draw him inside her by the sheer power of her glance. He did not wait any longer. Swinging up on his arms, he positioned himself precisely, knowing that she neither could nor would give him much help. Then as her thighs spread apart again by another reflex, he slid down and into her.

There was a short tugging, then a sudden easing as he broke through. She gave a short, sharp cry, then her tight wetness closed around him, so suddenly that it was his turn to gasp. He knew he had to hold back particularly long with Ye-Jaza, for bringing her to climax would be harder than usual. But knowing this and doing it were two different things. Very different, when she was writhing under him, clutching him with her arms and the more intimate parts of her body.

It seemed forever before that body's reaction came. And when it came, it was with an almost terrifying violence. Ye-Jaza sobbed and howled and clawed at Blade's back until blood ran from the gouges her nails made, thrashing and heaving and jerking under him. With the final shudder of her tormented pelvic muscles her eyes rolled up in her head, and she fainted. It was as if thirty years of virginity had built up a monstrous accumulation of energy, all ready to be discharged in that one moment.

But if Ye-Jaza released all her energy then, she regained it soon enough. And she found more than Blade had imagined she—or any woman—could. It was three entire days before she left Blade's chambers. By that time both she and Blade were a little unsteady on their feet. It had not taken Ye-Jaza more than her first experience of love for her to become an addict. Specifically, an addict to Blade.

Now this was all well and good up to a point, for it gave

Blade all the influence over her that he had ever dreamed of having. But she insisted that he promise to return to the Tower of the Leopard after the liberation of the Tower of the Serpent. She wanted him always around her, beside her—and in her.

Again, this was all very well and good, for the moment. But Blade strongly suspected that Mir-Kasa, if she survived the war, would make the same request. He could perhaps look forward to being caught in a tug-of-war between two strong-minded, able, and jealous women.

But that would be after the war. In the meantime that war had to be fought and won. And Blade had accomplished the crucial part of his mission, whatever difficulties he might have landed himself in during the process. Ye-Jaza remained as stubborn and proud toward everybody else as she had ever been. But she was putty in Blade's hands. And she gave her consent to the war against the Tower of the Serpent.

CHAPTER EIGHTEEN

It was just after dawn, the same time of day that Blade had arrived in Melnon. And the weather was almost the same also—a glowing blue sky overhead, promising a clear day— but the towers themselves were still veiled in mist. The towers—and the Waste Lands of the Tower of the Serpent, where five hundred picked fighting men crouched, waiting.

They had not been picked as carefully as Blade would have liked. But he could hardly argue that the refugees from the Tower of the Serpent should not be allowed to help liberate their home. And three hundred or more of the best fighting men of the Tower of the Leopard should balance any weaknesses among the exiles. There were also the two hundred "underground" fighters already inside the Tower of the Serpent. Blade and Bryg-Noz were hurling against Nris-Pol the strongest fighting force seen in Melnon in better than two hundred years. And it would get stronger still, the moment the pikes that each man was carrying got into the hands of the Low People. The attackers were carrying enough of those pikes to arm nearly every able-bodied Low Person in the Tower of the Serpent.

So they had strength and courage and determination. But skill, and the subtle battle sense that tells you when to strike and when to wait for a better time—did they have these also? Blade looked up at the sun. He would find out in a few minutes.

Blade locked at the Waste Land around him. No one looking casually down from the balcony at it would have dreamed that five hundred men lay hidden there, ready to strike. In fact, even someone looking for the men would have had trouble finding them. All their weapons and faces were smeared with brown-gray paste, and everyone wore faded green. The exiles from the Tower of the Serpent, of course, wore green by right. But it had been a struggle to get the Leopard warriors to wear something other than their own proud—and highly visible—yellow orange. Some of their commanders had even tried to invoke the War Wisdom in protest, until the Council of Leaders squelched them.

Blade could hardly think of a more pointless objection than the War Wisdom. After today's battle the War Wisdom and the Peace Wisdom alike would be shattered into small pieces, regardless of who won the battle. The old mold which had held Melnon in frozen suspension for centuries was about to come apart. Neither queens nor councils nor commanders would be able to put it back together again.

The mist was beginning to burn off under the heat of the fast-rising sun. Blade risked a look upward, to see if any signs of the war party's moving out showed on the balcony high above. He hoped they would hurry. He wanted the hundred warriors well on their way toward the Plain of War before people inside the tower launched their attack. The war party would certainly fight, otherwise. And to start off the day with a pitched battle against a hundred of Nris-Pol's opponents was not his choice.

The figures of men were beginning to appear along the railing of the balcony now. Not very many of them, though, at least not yet. The sacred routine set by the War Wisdom would prevail even today—at least for a few more minutes.

Blade was wearing the usual two swords in their scabbards and a stout club hanging on his belt. He also carried a great wand, wrapped in cloth and slung on his back. That was strictly for the worst sort of life-or-death emergency. Bryg-Noz and Blade alike felt that it would be far better to get through the entire day's fighting without revealing the great wands any more than necessary. Their existence would be enough of a shock to the people of the tower if it was announced peacefully, after the fighting was over. Unleashing them in the middle of the battle could also unleash utter chaos.

More figures were appearing on the balcony. Still no sign of any change from the usual routine, or of any awareness of danger. One man was visibly standing a little apart from his fellows. Then Blade saw the gleam of a lifter dropping down, to swing just in front of the man. The First on the Ground launched himself downward. In a few minutes he was indeed on the ground. Blade heard the familiar words of the formal declaration faintly across the hundred yards to the base of the tower.

Then men started swinging themselves out into space on lifters and plunging downward. Blade felt his own breath quicken, and felt a tension almost radiating from the forty-odd men scattered across the Waste Land around him. They were primarily a diversionary force, to fight only if there was no other way to keep the war party busy. Their main goal was the balcony, and a rendezvous with the main attack.

It would not be long now. More than half the war party was already on the ground, and Blade could count a dozen warriors descending on lifters at any one moment. Sixty, seventy, eighty—the number of men on the ground swelled continuously.

And then there was a sudden soundless flurry of motion among the figures remaining on the balcony, and the glint of dancing swords catching the sun. One of the figures was forced against the railing, and then over it. The dark shape plunged down through two hundred feet of air, his limbs flailing desperately. A small puff of dust rose where he struck the earth. A moment later another came sailing down after it, and a moment later two more. One of the last seemed to be wearing the work clothes of one of the Low People, but even Blade's eagle-sharp eyes could not be certain.

157

But he could be certain that something had gone badly wrong with the attack inside the tower. It was supposed to strike upward from the lowest Levels to the balcony, clear it, then lower the lifters for the men on the ground outside. That way the whole attack would not have to fight its way up the narrow stairs, where the defending warriors would have all the advantages. But the attack was not supposed to start until after the war party was well on its way to the Plain of War. Someone had blundered, and the alarm was up. Blade cursed under his breath.

A moment later someone else blundered. This time it was one of Blade's own men. Forgetting to wait for Blade's signal, he rose from his hiding place and hurled his smoke bomb. This time Blade swore out loud, in a bellowing roar that rolled away across the Waste Land. Plumes of green smoke suddenly spurted up on either side of him in response to the first bomb, as the scouts relayed the message. Blade's straining ears could pick out war cries on the other side of the tower as the main attacking party rose from its cover and moved into action.

He wasted no more breath swearing. The damage was done. Now all he could do was to try to salvage as much as possible—perhaps even a victory. Blade himself rose from cover, snatched a smoke bomb from the sack at his waist, and hurled it as far as he could toward the war party. Thick, oily green smoke gushed up, spreading fast across his field of vision, mixing with the mist to form an impenetrable curtain.

Seeing Blade in action, his other forty warriors joined in. The war party vanished behind a solid wall of rolling, greasy green smoke. The wall spread to either side, and forward and backward as well. Within moments of the first bomb, gentle swirling greenness was all around Blade. With luck, both his own men and the war party would be completely invisible from the balcony. The men up there would have no idea of what was happening on the ground.

He dipped into the bag again, pulled out a white armband, and tied it about his left arm. With everybody on both sides wearing green, some sort of identification was needed to distinguish attackers from defenders. Blade hoped that all his men would remember this precaution. If they didn't, on their own heads be it. He wasn't going to stop to ask questions.

Then he pulled out a whistle, put it to his lips, and blew— hard. The mist and the smoke and his own taut nerves did weird things to the whistle blast. It seemed to go on and on, echoing from the walls of all seven towers like some terrible death-shriek. But from behind Blade and on either side of him came the sound of running feet. Dim figures pounded past in the smoke, heading for the tower and the war party. The warriors of Melnon were accustomed to fighting duels, not pitched battles. So the warriors of the Serpent would have no training to help them stand off a massed attack. Nor did the warriors of the Leopard have much training to help them deliver one. Blade hoped surprise and speed and the smokescreen would let them get away with it, however. He drew his own two swords and broke into a run.

Blade wore light sandals, like the rest of his men, and he skimmed lightly over the broken ground. But others ran even faster. Before Blade had covered half the distance to the base of the tower, war-cries and death-cries and the clang of weapons sounded from ahead.

Blade charged through a thick patch of smoke and came out in the middle of the fight. A small wiry figure darted at him, with his long sword reaching out. There was no flash of white on the man's arm. Blade parried by reflex and struck by calculation. His short sword drove into the man so hard that it penetrated through the armor and into the flesh. Blood spurted down the glossy green, and the man howled in agony and reeled back.

He reeled into the path of one of Blade's men, forcing him to halt for a moment. A long sword swished out of the smoke and took the exile's head clean off. But that in turn slowed the man with the long sword long enough for Blade to close under his guard and kick him in the groin. The man doubled up, and as he did so, Blade's long sword came down. A second head flew into the air, to bounce and roll to a stop not far from the first.

That was the first and last exchange of blows that Blade remembered at all clearly. From the moment the second head struck the ground, the battle dissolved and flowed around him in an endless confusion of rushing bodies, flashing swords, and screaming men. He remembered losing his short sword to a down-cut from an oversized warrior, closing with the man, and chopping him across the throat with a knife-hand karate blow. He remembered tripping over a body that suddenly rolled under his feet, and rolling in his turn to escape the down-slash of a long sword. Then he sprang to his feet behind the attacker, closed, locked both hands around the man's head, and jerked back hard to snap his neck like a carrot.

He even remembered shouting, "Hold! Warriors of the Tower of the Serpent, hold! We come only to destroy Nris-Pol, a danger to us all! We are not your enemies!" But nobody in the war party believed him. He didn't really expect them to.

Eventually both the smoke and the fighting began to break up. Some of the survivors of the war party ran blindly off into the Waste Land, pursued by some of Blade's survivors. Others, less panic-stricken, ran to their lifters and began to rise into the air.

But Blade had planned for this also. Several of his men ran forward, swinging weighted lines. They whirled the lines about their heads, then sent them whipping upward. The weights looped around the lifter cords, tangling them. Before the men on the lifters could react, the men on the ground had fastened their cords to stout pegs. A few hefty blows with a mallet drove each peg into the ground. And then it was just a tug of war between the reel above and the peg below.

Usually it was the reel that lost. They were not designed to cope with the extra strain. One by one they burnt out, and let their lifters fall. Some of the men on the lifters survived the falls long enough for Blade's men to have to fight them. But Blade saw one warrior come straight down from forty feet up. He writhed about like a half-severed worm, his back obviously broken. Blade went over to him and put him out of his misery with the short sword.

As Blade stepped back from the stiffening body, a pike sailed down from above, slicing into the earth with a thump six feet away. He glared upward for a moment, then he noticed that a slip of white paper was fastened to the butt of the pike. He picked it up and read:

Balcony secured. Main attack force getting into position. Join us as soon as possible. Bryg-Noz.

The signature was unmistakable. Blade turned to his men and shouted, "We've got the balcony. They'll be sending down lifters for us in a moment. Everybody follow me."

The war party was no threat any more. Half its members were dead or maimed, the other half either fleeing or fled, and demoralized by the sudden nightmare attack out of the greenness. By the time they recovered their nerve, if they ever did, the main battle in the tower would have been decided one way or the other.

Blade waited as the lifters came down one by one, and his unwounded men scrambled into them and rose up toward the balcony. The smoke was almost gone now, and he could see that the railing far above was lined with a motley array of figures. A good many of them were carrying pikes.

When the last of his men had gone, Blade climbed into a lifter of his own. The cord tightened, and the lifter lurched and swayed sickeningly up into the air. Blade held on and swallowed. The battle had not affected him at all—he had seen much worse many times. But the pendulum motion of a rapidly-rising lifter was something he was never going to get used to, no matter how long he stayed in Melnon.

CHAPTER NINETEEN

Bryg-Noz met Blade as the Englishman climbed out of his lifter on to the balcony. The Melnonian's right arm was wrapped in a crude bandage caked with rust-colored dried blood, but he seemed steady enough on his feet. Certainly his voice was clear enough as he summed up the situation. Practically the whole attacking force was up, and the lifters and reels were being temporarily disabled.

"Why?" asked Blade.

"We don't want any of Nris-Pol's men escaping to other towers. And we don't want any of the other towers sending men over to help Nris-Pol. We want to fight this out among ourselves."

Blade nodded. "What about the pikes and the Low People?"

"Over a thousand of them have already been armed. We are holding them back for the moment."

"Why the devil are you doing that?" snapped Blade. "We've got to move fast. There isn't any time for fussing about details, or trying to keep the Low People under control." He clapped his hands together suddenly as a thought struck him, so loudly that Bryg-Noz jumped in surprise.

"What is it, Blade-Liza?"

"Are the shafts still working?"

"Yes."

"Good. That means Nris-Pol still doesn't realize how big an attack this is. Otherwise he'd shut off the shafts and let us try fighting our way up the stairs one level at a time. That could take weeks. But with the shafts still running..." Blade turned away, a frown on his face as his mind ran over the possibilities and the risks. Then he turned back to Bryg-Noz. "Can you give me fifty of your best fighters?"

"Fifty? What for?"

"I want to go up the queen's shaft to the queen's chambers and try to take and hold them."

Bryg-Noz's jaw dropped, but he managed to close it as Blade raced on. "Mir-Kasa is something that Nris-Pol is going to have to defend. Even if he doesn't want to, the warriors will probably do it without his orders, or even against them. Unless, of course, he is planning to kill her..." He saw Bryg-Noz shudder at the thought.

"Either way, my attack should draw a few hundred of Nris-Pol's fighters up to a higher level. There may not be enough left to even hold the stairs, particularly if you let the Low People loose."

"Let the Low People loose?" echoed Bryg-Noz. "They will—"

"I know perfectly well what they'll do." Both time and his temper were getting shorter. He raised a hand to mop the sweat off his forehead. "But you've already done most of the damage, by making the attack in the first place. Are you going to hold back from one more step, one that might give you victory, and let all you've done so far be wasted? Are you going to let Kun-Rala's death be a waste?"

That shaft struck home. Bryg-Noz winced, and for a moment Blade could see the man's lower lip trembling. Bryg-Noz's voice was half-choked as he nodded and said almost in a whisper, "And perhaps you will save Mir-Kasa herself, too." There must have been real affection between them once, Blade realized.

Blade did not have much time to think about Bryg-Noz's feelings. Word of what he wanted had spread around the balcony almost instantly. Men swarmed around Blade, clamoring to be chosen to join him. He could not help being moved by this sign of his reputation, particularly when he was leading them on what might well turn out to be a suicide mission.

With the fifty men behind him, Blade dashed toward the queen's shaft. He knew the shaft cars were large enough to hold at least twenty-five men and still give them room to breathe and even use their weapons. He sent the other half of his party around to the shaft of the warriors, with orders to get off at the level of the queen's chambers. He didn't like dividing his forces this way, but it was either that or try walking up three thousand feet of stairs. And Blade wanted his men to arrive in shape to fight.

The shaft door opened as Blade led the head of his column toward it. He drew both swords, but stopped dead as the First Warrior himself led a column of his own out of the car, into the corridor. Then it was the First Warrior's turn to stop, stare, and shout to the men still in the car.

Blade tossed his short sword into the air, caught it by the tip, and threw it. It drove through the armor of a man just stepping out of the car door. He clutched at the sword suddenly standing out from his stomach, gave a choked, gurgling cry, and collapsed to the floor. His body blocked the track of the door, jamming it open as the men inside struggled to close it. One of them bent to drag the body free. Blade charged, long sword raised high. It came down, and the bending man's head lolled hideously. Now there were two bodies jamming the door open, and the men inside the car gave up the effort to close the door. They drew their swords and poured out around Blade, yelling incoherently as much in fear as in anger. Their wide staring eyes and gaping mouths made an ugly sight.

But they were too furious or too frightened to be very good swordsmen. None of their wild slashes came anywhere near Blade. He backed away, and as he did so, his own men charged forward and swirled around the defenders. The defenders were outnumbered almost two to one, apart from being frightened half out of their wits. Six of them went down in as many seconds.

The First Warrior made no effort to draw his sword or defend himself otherwise. So none of Blade's men considered him dangerous, or even worth attacking. He stayed alive a little bit longer than the rest of his men, and even began to edge away down the corridor, with his eyes roaming about in a frantic search for escape. Then a great yelling and screaming split the air. Hard behind it came the sound of running feet, as a swarm of Low People came charging down the corridor, brandishing pikes. The First Warrior had just time to throw up his hands and scream—"N-n-noooooooo!"—before the Low People were on him. They knew his love for administering Low People very well. By the time they had finished shoving their pikes into his body, the First Warrior was a mangled mess, lying in the middle of a spreading pool of blood.

Blade took in the sight briefly, considering what it meant. If the people above had sent the First Warrior himself down to lead the counterattack—well, their notions of what was going on below must be even more confused than Blade had thought. And he was going to strike before they had time to sort things out.

He led his men into the shaft car and sent it hurtling upward without even giving them time to brace themselves. Several were thrown off balance, went sprawling, and had to struggle to their feet.

As they neared the level of the queen's chambers, Blade called out, "When the door opens—charge! Hit them hard, before the bastards wake up to what's happening. We want to put them all to sleep before they do!" Grim laughter filled the car, and with it the rasp of swords being drawn. Then Blade felt the car slowing. The car slowed further, stopped— and the door hissed open.

Blade's twenty-five men charged out of the car with a fury that would have made ten times their number give ground.

They screamed, they shouted, they hurled curses and the filthiest epithets they could think of, and they brandished their swords in glittering arcs. There were barely thirty men in the corridor facing them at that moment. Blade's charge smashed into those men like a battering ram.

Most of the thirty went down on to the floor in the first few moments. Not all of these were dead, or even wounded. The sheer physical impact of Blade's charging men swept a good number of the enemy off their feet. But if they were alive and unwounded when they went down, they seldom got to their feet that way. Blade and his men were all over them, slashing and stabbing. They kicked and stamped as well, and armor that could turn a sword could not always keep ribs from collapsing under the crushing force of a boot. The floor became littered with an increasing number of dead bodies, and the space between the bodies slowly became red and slippery with blood. Almost before Blade had time to realize it, the first defenders were down, dead, or running for their lives.

But these were far from the only warriors Nris-Pol had on the level, as Blade discovered a moment later. In fact, it seemed that Nris-Pol was keeping his main reserves around the queen's chambers. The other shaft door hissed open, Blade's other twenty-five men poured out—and then the enemy's counterattack came thundering down the corridor nearly a hundred strong.

It caught Blade's second group before it could deploy. Now it was the turn of Blade's men to be swept away or slaughtered before they could form battle lines. Screams, shouts, and the clash of weapons rose in a deafening pandemonium. A few of the twenty-five managed to run and join Blade's own group, but most died where they stood. In dying, though, they gave Blade the chance to reform his own men into a solid line. Not much time, but enough so that when Nris-Pol's attack came boiling down the corridor again, Blade could meet them. He met them with his swords dancing, and bellowing at the top of his lungs, "For a free tower! Down with Nris-Pol!" Then the two forces collided, pandemonium rose again, and Blade could no longer keep track of what was happening around him.

Blade suddenly found himself having to be in six places at once, leading counterattacks, shoring up his sagging line, worrying about what might happen if his men were taken in the rear. Occasionally he had the satisfaction of feeling his sword sinking deeply into an opponent, and seeing a gap in the other formation instead of his own. But the odds against his men were long to start with, and they got longer in spite of all that Blade could do. Soon there were only twenty-two of his men left, then eighteen, then sixteen. The enemy was still coming onward with sixty or more. Bit by bit, Blade led his dwindling numbers backward, away from the queen's chambers. He knew that he was leaving Mir-Kasa vulnerable, that his own death was perhaps only a few minutes away. But he was determined to keep himself and as many of his men as he could alive and fighting for as long as they could breathe and move and lift their swords.

The battle rose to a new peak, and then a totally new set of noises reached Blade's ear. The sound of running feet and sword-strokes was coming now from the *rear* of the attackers. Mixed with those were shouts of "Treason! Treason!" and then other shouts of "Mir-Kasa!"

Somebody was hitting Nris-Pol's men hard from the rear, and Blade would have given an arm—or at least a few fingers—to have known who it was. But he could see with his own eyes that Nris-Pol's warriors stopped their advance, looked nervously over their shoulders, and began to turn. The warriors directly opposite Blade's shrunken band began to step back and lower their swords. Blade made a quick decision, then stepped two paces out in front of his men. Again he raised his swords—now battered and blood-caked—and raised his voice to a roar.

"At them!" And he charged at the enemy's lines without

bothering to look back to see whether his men would follow. He had been through enough with them this day to be sure that they would.

They did. The sixteen warriors, reeking of sweat and dripping blood, struck the enemy only seconds behind Blade. They struck before the warriors in the enemy's first rank could get ready to defend themselves. So that first rank and the two ranks behind it dissolved in confusion under the charge. Some of its warriors fought, some stepped aside, a few simply turned and ran.

Or at least they tried to run. Attacked from before and behind, Nris-Pol's men were now being packed tighter and tighter together. The mass of them filled the corridor from side to side, offering no room for a man to run and little room for a man to use his weapons. Blade and his men were hacking their way slowly into that mass, meeting less and less resistance each minute as panic began spreading through the enemy's ranks. Down the corridor Blade could see the line of swords approaching slowly, as the men still shouting "Mir-Kasa" did the same.

Eventually the two forces met. The greater part of Nris-Pol's men had died where they stood, but some had surrendered, throwing their swords on the floor and kneeling in submission. They seemed stunned and bewildered by what had happened, except for one or two who glared at Blade defiantly as he went around tying their hands behind their backs. One of them muttered, "Wait until our leader returns and steps forth among you. Then you bastards won't be walking so proudly!"

Blade did not have time to speculate on what this muttering might mean. One of the warriors from the other attacking force ran up to him and clutched at his arm. "Blade-Liza! Blade-Liza! Kir-Noz would speak with you. Come quickly, for he is dying!"

Blade thrust both swords back in their scabbards and hurried after the man. They found Kir-Noz a little way down the corridor, propped up against the wall of a small alcove.

168

Blood trickled from his mouth, in startling contrast to the whiteness of his skin. One glance was enough to tell Blade that the messenger was right. Kir-Noz had only a few minutes to live.

"How—how is my brother?" asked the warrior. His voice was low but clear. It seemed that he was putting all of his fading strength into making it so.

"He is wounded, but he will live to rule in the Tower of the Serpent."

"Good. I hope so. You—must find—Nris-Pol. There is a room—in the Work Chambers—"

Blade's insides turned to ice. Had Nris-Pol found the great wands? He wanted to ask that question. But he found his dry tongue sticking to the roof of his mouth.

Kir-Noz answered the unasked question. "He says—a new weapon—there. Will kill—everybody against him. You first—he hates you like he does—Mir-Kasa."

"How is Mir-Kasa?" asked Blade urgently.

"Took—poison," murmured Kir-Noz. "She—is—dead." Kir-Noz's head lolled sideways, and in a moment he, too, was dead.

CHAPTER TWENTY

Blade stepped back from the dead warrior and made the formal hand gestures of respect for one of the honored dead. He sighed. If Bryg-Noz in fact came to rule in the Tower of the Serpent, he would rule as a very lonely man. His brother, Mir-Kasa, Kun-Rala—they were all dead. Blade took another step back from the body, and turned back toward his men, to watch them dragging the prisoners to their feet and piling the bodies out of the way.

That extra step saved Blade's life. As he took it, there was a sudden hiss and crackle of disturbed air behind him. He spun around, in time to see one of the men farther down the corridor vanish in a cloud of red mist that stained the floor where he had been standing. Instantly Blade leaped into the alcove where Kir-Noz's body was and flattened himself against the wall. As he did that, the air crackled again, and another man became a red cloud in the heavy air of the corridor.

As he struggled to get his own great wand out of its bag and into action, Blade's mind was working furiously. How many men with great wands had Nris-Pol brought up into action? And was Nris-Pol himself among them? Blade very much hoped so.

A third crackle, and a third stain on the floor. And then the men in the corridor broke, abandoning the prisoners, abandoning Blade, abandoning the ground they had won, to vanish in a mad panicky flight. They could face three times their own number of enemy warriors with courage, but not the great wands.

As his men clattered off down the corridor, Blade could take comfort from at least two things. There seemed to be only one man with a great wand, and the great wand could fire only in a straight line. Blade's opponent could not fire at him without giving Blade some chance to return the fire. With luck, Blade had only to stay where he was, and wait for curiosity or blood-lust to tempt his enemy out into view. He let his breath out slowly, trying to relax as much as possible without losing any of his alertness.

A minute went by. Then two minutes, then three. The corridor—in fact, the whole level—seemed as silent as a tomb. As far as Blade's ears could tell, there was no other living thing on the level or in the corridor with him.

It must have been close to ten minutes before he heard the unmistakable sound of a footstep—a single slow, cautious footstep. After an interval that seemed like hours, it was followed by a second. Now they came in more rapid succession, approaching down the corridor. Blade could not keep from holding his breath. Then he let it out in a soundless gasp, as Nris-Pol himself came into view around the bend of the corridor.

Blade stepped out into the open, his great wand rising into position as he did so. Before Nris-Pol's widening eyes could meet his, his finger squeezed down on the firing bar. And it squeezed in vain, as the bar jammed fast.

Before Nris-Pol could even realize Blade's situation, let alone gloat over it, Blade had reacted. It was his habit to learn every possible way of using any weapon he might be given, however unlikely he might be to need it. He had practiced throwing the great wands—and also using them butt-first. They weighed fifteen pounds, and coming down hard, butt-end first, they could do their share of damage.

So as Nris-Pol's wand rose to aim at Blade and Nris-Pol's finger tightened on his own firing bar, Blade sprang at the

171

other man. He lifted his wand, then brought it down. By pure reflex Nris-Pol jerked his wand up enough to spoil Blade's stroke at his head. The two wands met with a clang of metal and a jar that nearly knocked Blade's out of his hands. But it did knock Nris-Pol's wand out of his. The wand crashed to the floor, and Blade closed, raising his own wand for a finishing stroke to cave Nris-Pol's skull in.

That stroke came down on empty air. Nris-Pol's skull was no longer where Blade had expected it to be. Fast on his feet, the warrior sprang away from Blade, turned, and ran. Blade followed him. He had little doubt where Nris-Pol was headed. He had even less doubt that thousands of lives might depend on stopping him. If the man had brought out the great wands, had he noticed Kun-Rala's little trap? Perhaps. And perhaps he was now heading that way, determined that if he could not rule in the Tower of the Serpent, no one should.

Blade ran fast, but he had been fighting since early morning. Nris-Pol ran faster. Blade saw the warrior's fleeting shape dart through the door of one of the shafts, then he saw the light go on as the shaft car plunged downward. Without stopping or even swearing, Blade continued on around the corridor to the next shaft car. By miraculous good fortune the car was only a few levels above; a push of the button brought it down to him within seconds. He sprang in, and another push of the button sent it plunging downward. But he was almost a minute behind Nris-Pol, and a few seconds would be more than enough for the desperate warrior.

Blade found it hard to keep from holding his breath as the car shot downward. He found it even harder to worry about there being hostile warriors in or around the work chambers. He would fight his way through them, or around them—somehow. He would get to Nris-Pol—somehow. He realized that he was not thinking quite rationally, and took deep breaths to calm himself. He had just managed to do so when the car stopped and the shaft door opened.

Blade knew the way to the work chambers, so he had no need to look around him. He came out of the shaft car at a dead run, bowling over two masters armed with administering wands as though he were an avalanche. They sprawled on the floor, staring after him as he pounded down the corridor.

Blade had dropped his useless great wand on the floor of the shaft car so that he could run unhampered. But Nris-Pol still managed to keep ahead of him. Blade could hear the pounding feet ahead, and could hear them slowly getting louder as he carved away Nris-Pol's lead. But he could not come up with Nris-Pol before the man ducked into the chamber where the store of great wands lay. And he did not dare charge straight into the chamber on Nris-Pol's heels. The man could easily get himself another great wand and be ready to blast Blade into a red mist if he came charging in. So once more Blade flattened himself against a wall, then peered cautiously around the edge of the doorway into the chamber.

The door in the wall gaped blackly open, and Nris-Pol was on his knees on the floor. He was holding the bunch of power tubes in one hand, and doing something to the wires with the other. Or trying to do something, at least. Blade could hear Nris-Pol's frustrated, half-hysterical cursing, and let his own breath out in a sigh of relief. Somehow something had gone wrong with the wiring of Kun-Rala's boobytrap. At any other time that might have been a disaster, but now it was salvation for the Tower of the Serpent. Nris-Pol had found the great wands too late, and been too afraid of handing them out to his men. Now he was going to pay for both mistakes. Blade stepped out into the middle of the doorway and launched himself into the chamber.

He had made a mistake of his own, however. Only a small one, but still a mistake. He had thought Nris-Pol a hysterical, half-helpless madman. But as Blade charged, Nris-Pol spun around, snatched up a heavy metal tool from the floor, and hurled it straight at Blade. Blade leaped high, but the tool smashed into the side of his right knee. Pain knifed through his leg, and he nearly fell to the floor as he came down. He raised both swords, though, and took an agonized, lurching step forward.

Nris-Pol could have killed Blade in that moment. But the sight of Blade coming at him was too much for his overstrained nerves. This time they did snap, and he gave a wild animal's scream. Then he dashed for the door, brushing past Blade and under Blade's sword-slashes, and out of the chamber.

Blade turned and followed him. Somewhere he came up with the strength to run, in spite of the pain in his knee and his weariness from the fighting. Not only to run, but to run fast. He was only a few steps behind the fleeing Nris-Pol as they sprinted out of the work chambers into the corridor leading to the shafts.

As they reached the doors of the shafts, a tremendous rumble echoed down the corridor. Floors and walls and ceiling all heaved and shook, sprinkling the running men with bits of debris. All the indicator lights over the shaft doors went out, and some of them exploded, spraying bits of glass on to the floor.

Blade did not need Nris-Pol's howl of fury to tell him what had happened. Somewhere, high above or far below, somebody had violently cut off the power to the shafts. They would need stairs to get up and down the tower for the rest of the battle.

Nris-Pol was heading for the door to the nearest stairway before the echoes of the power cut-off had stopped rolling through the corridor. He plunged through the door and on down the stairs still a few steps ahead of Blade. If he had stopped to fight, he might have been able to beat Blade off, or perhaps hold him long enough for others of his own men to come up. But there was no more reasoning left in him than there was in a mad dog. All he could think of was to get away from the towering blood-stained figure pounding along after him, swords drawn and gleaming.

They went down the stairs at a dead run. Blade's breath

was beginning to be a white-hot rasping in his lungs. His legs felt as though they were made of rubber, and his knee sent pains stabbing up into his brain each time his right foot slammed down on a step. Once he nearly stumbled and went headlong down the stairs on top of the fugitive ahead. Several times he heard scrabbling feet and panicky whimpers that suggested Nris-Pol also had nearly fallen. But the man was always able to stay on his feet, somehow, and even keep his distance.

Nris-Pol was still out in the lead when the five-hundred foot stairway ended, and the two men dashed out into a corridor on the level of the balcony. Nris-Pol threw a wild-eyed glance over his shoulder at Blade, and lurched away in the direction of the balcony itself. Blade followed him. He noticed some of Bryg-Noz's warriors and armed Low People passing by. Part of his mind told him he should call out to them, tell them to seize Nris-Pol. But the other part told him that this was between him and Nris-Pol, and that it should stay that way.

Then they were out on the balcony itself, and Nris-Pol was heading for the railing without slowing down. He did not slow down as he reached the railing and slammed hard up against it—and then went over. Nor did he scream as he went over. He plunged the two hundred feet down to the ground in silence.

That silence was not broken until he landed. Blade had just reached the railing when that happened. On the ground far below a searing burst of purple flame shot up, rising upward and outward in all directions like a huge and hideous flower. Then it faded, and a thick cloud of greasy black smoke puffed up, hiding a wide patch of ground. After a few moments the light breeze cleared away the smoke, and Blade could get a clear view of the scene below. Where Nris-Pol had struck there was now a crater a good ten feet wide and five feet deep, with charred earth banked up around its edges. Several bodies were lying on the ground around the crater. Farther away, people were lying on the ground and moving feebly, or sitting up slowly and rubbing their heads.

The fall of Nris-Pol did not immediately lead to the fall of the Tower of the Serpent. But it certainly eased things considerably, as the defenders discovered that their leader was dead. They also discovered that the Low People were roaming about the tower with pikes in their hands, sticking those pikes into any of the High People they found. The defenders' morale fell, and so did their swords. Well before the dinner hour, all resistance had ceased. Within an hour after that, Bryg-Noz's men and their Low People allies had occupied the whole tower and had even managed to get the shafts operating again..

Blade took over the First Warrior's chambers as his own personal command post. From its windows he watched the sun go down over Melnon, the towers to the west looming black and huge against the glow of the sunset. There were many more night-lights on the other towers than usual. This did not surprise him at all. They would certainly be spending a sleepless night tonight. Nor would this be the last one, either. But both the Tower of the Leopard and the Tower of the Serpent had alert guards posted. They would not be surprised and destroyed, tonight or any other night. And because they would not be destroyed, the old way in Melnon was gone forever.

Blade had just reached the point of realizing that he was horribly hungry when a Leopard warrior he knew came into the chambers. He bore a message from Ye-Jaza, on her perfumed stationery. To Blade, the perfume seemed grotesquely out of place, considering that he had been smelling nothing but blood and sweat all day. But he opened the letter, and a sour smile curled his lips as he read it. Then he threw it on the floor.

"What is it, honored Blade-Liza?" asked the warrior.

"Ye-Jaza wants to come over and join me—tonight—here in the Tower of the Serpent. She wants to see what has been done, she says."

"She wants an easy thrill," said the warrior sourly. His

armor was slashed and there was blood on his legs. He had fought his fair share that day, and had the same opinion of thrill-seeking spectators as Blade did.

"She's asking the impossible," said Blade. "I'll have to tell her that."

The warrior shook his head wearily. "I would not call that wise, Blade-Liza. Ye-Jaza is of the type to be jealous—madly jealous. If you do not let her come over, she will think you are with another woman. And then—" the warrior shrugged.

Blade sighed. He would have cursed, if he had felt strong enough to do it. "I know. She will do her best to get the alliance of the two towers broken up."

"Yes. And perhaps she might even try to have you killed. That would be a terrible tragedy for Melnon, if I may say so What you have done—not just today, but—"

"I know, I know. We'll talk about that later. I suppose I had better let her come over. You can tell her that. But be sure to pick a few reliable warriors to escort her over. I'm damned if I want her run through with a pike by some roving Low Person who doesn't recognize her."

The warrior nodded and left without another word. Blade leaned wearily back in his chair. Why not? he thought. Mir-Kasa was dead, and so was Kun-Rala. There was no other woman in Melnon now for him except Ye-Jaza. It would be comparatively easy to keep her happy, and the alliance intact. And she was far from bad company, when all was said and done, particularly now that thirty years of obstinate virginity had been swept away and dumped on the garbage heap.

There was another knock on the door. "Come in," he called absently. The door opened, and four warriors half-pushed, half-pulled the First Surgeon of the Tower of the Serpent into the room.

Blade rose, his mouth starting to fall open in surprise before he caught himself. "This is—unexpected," he managed to say. "I expected that you would be killed."

"Well, I was not." The First Surgeon seemed much more

in control of himself than he had been, the day Blade saw him trembling at Mir-Kasa's coming. "Nor were many of the other surgeons and scribes and workers. We managed to lock ourselves away in our chambers. But we will come out if you can offer us safety from the Low People. In fact—" the Surgeon hesitated "—we will even work for you, and Bryg-Noz, if you will treat us well."

Fatigue made Blade too foggy-minded to completely grasp what the surgeon meant at first. Then realization hit him. "Why?" he snapped suddenly.

The Surgeon flinched, but did not back away. "What you have done today—in the Tower of the Serpent—it cannot be undone. Many have already died. More will die if nothing is done. What is the sense of that?" The surgeon shrugged. "We are defeated. The surgeons and scribes at least have the wit to know that." He sagged into a chair, as though his knees would no longer keep him on his feet.

Blade remained standing, his mind turning in slow circles. Cooperation from any of the High People was the last thing that either he or Bryg-Noz had expected. But if it was going to be forthcoming, if the First Surgeon was speaking for others besides himself—well, Bryg-Noz's job was going to be a damned sight easier! Blade flexed his shoulders to get some of the kinks out of them, then nodded slowly. "Very well. I accept your offer. Warriors, take this man to Bryg-Noz. It is proper that he have the final word." The escort moved in to hustle the surgeon out, but as they did the man raised a warning hand.

"Wait, I have something else for you!"

"Yes?"

"A message from Queen Mir-Kasa."

Blade sat down again abruptly. "Queen Mir-Kasa? But she is dead!"

The surgeon smiled rather nervously and shook his head. "It was only a drug that produces a sleep so deep one can easily mistake it for death. I gave it to her this morning, when the battle started, so that Nris-Pol would not seek her out and kill her. She is waking now, and wants to see you." Then the warriors hustled the surgeon out, before he could say anything more.

Blade also could not say anything more for a while. Then he said "Damn!" in a loud voice. He was not exactly sorry that Mir-Kasa was alive, but it was going to complicate things rather horribly. Could he send another message to Ye-Jaza, telling her not to come? Possibly, but what good would that do? And how much harm might it not do?

No, he would just have to take the shaft back up to the Queen's Chambers, and explain the situation to Mir-Kasa. She was older, more experienced. Perhaps she was wiser, and just conceivably she might be more tolerant of this kind of situation. That wouldn't help things in the long run, but it might keep him out of trouble tonight—unless of course Ye-Jaza wanted love-making that he was far too exhausted to give. And she probably would want just that.

There were times when Blade could appreciate the advantages of a monastic life.

He rose wearily out of his chair and started toward the bathing chamber. Mir-Kasa could certainly wait at least until he got some of the grime and blood off him. Two of the Low People stepped toward him, to help him strip off his armor.

As they reached for him, it seemed that the ceiling above him split open with a roar. It was a roar so loud that it made white-hot pain explode in his head. For a moment he was blinded by that pain. In the moment of blackness it seemed that strong gusts of wind roared up around him, cold and terrible, lifting him up from the floor, through the gap in the ceiling. But he was not alarmed. The computer had reached out, grabbed him, was pulling him home, away from Melnon, its problems, and its jealous women.

The wind continued to roar as he hurtled upward. Level after level flashed past him, blurred now, for he was rising as fast as a shaft car. Then there were no more levels, and the wind was carrying him out through the very roof of the

Tower of the Serpent, up into the night over Melnon. For a long moment he saw the seven towers spread out below him in their great circle, their lights gleaming in the darkness. Then the cold came upon him again, and the darkness swallowed him, and the pain burst in his head again, and he stopped seeing anything.

CHAPTER TWENTY-ONE

Blade was out of the hospital bed and doing exercises when the nurse announced J and Lord Leighton. He climbed back into bed, favoring the right knee a little. It was almost fully back in shape, and there was no further reason for him to be kept in the hospital. But it was standard practice to whip him off to the small hospital in the underground complex whenever he returned from Dimension X. Sometimes—as after this trip—it had been more for observation, testing, and debriefing than anything else. But at other times he had returned from Dimension X with wounds or diseases that would have carried him off within hours or days.

Both J and Lord Leighton shook hands with him, and J looked him up and down with his usual air of fatherly concern. "How's the knee, Richard?"

"Almost back to normal, sir. No problem there."

"Good. You can get ready to leave the hospital, then, as soon as the doctors have given you a final once-over lightly. Then you can plan to take a few days off."

Blade raised an inquiring eyebrow. "I thought you were going to want me to help plan the new training center as soon as I got back."

Leighton shrugged. "Hardly necessary right at the moment. After all—I mean—we can't wear you out by not giving you some sort of vacation." Lord Leighton seemed oddly unsure of himself and of his words. Blade wondered what hidden message lay behind this rather unusual circumstance.

J grinned. "Now, now, old friend, let's be honest with Richard. He ought to know the whole story. Do you want to tell him, or shall I?"

There *was* something lurking behind Leighton's manner. Something that had interfered with the training-center project. Leighton smiled thinly, cleared his throat, and said:

"Actually, Richard, there's been a bit of a scandal in connection with the center."

Blade's eyebrows rose again, but this time his voice was coldly serious as he asked, "A security problem? Did somebody defect?"

"No, no, nothing like that. More—personal. You see, we had an architect all cleared and ready with plans for the restoration of the house. We could trust him completely. But unfortunately, our security check—MI6's security check—"

J threw a mock glare at Lord Leighton.

"— *the* security check, failed to reveal one thing about this—ah, gentleman."

"Yes?" prompted Blade. This was beginning to sound interesting.

"He was keeping a mistress—young girl, hardly out of her teens—down in Soho. And his wife found out. Damned distressing situation for her, you must admit."

"No doubt." But there was still more, from Leighton's tone of voice.

"It seems she trailed him down to Soho, and surprised him with the girl, and polished both of them off with the kitchen cleaver." The words came out in a rush, and Leighton took a deep breath and mopped his high forehead with a crumpled handkerchief.

"So the project is temporarily at a standstill," continued J. "We've been able to keep anything about the poor blighter's work out of the papers. But you can see, it's a deadly embarrassing situation."

Blade laughed loudly. "Yes, I can see it might be. Most of

all for the architect. Perhaps he should have volunteered for the Project. That computer of yours can come in handy for getting out from between jealous women."

Leighton and J both looked curiously at Blade. He realized that they must not have had a chance to listen to his debriefing tapes. So he explained the situation he had been in at the time of his return, caught between Mir-Kasa and Ye-Jaza. Leighton laughed briefly, J grinned even more briefly. "Glad we brought you back when we did, then."

"I'm glad to be back."

Which was certainly the truth.

the Executioner

PINNACLE BOOKS

The gutsiest, most exciting hero in years. Imagine a guy at war with the Godfather and all his Mafioso relatives! He's rough, he's deadly, he's a law unto himself — nothing and nobody stops him!

THE EXECUTIONER SERIES by DON PENDLETON

Order		Title	Book #	Price
————	# 1	WAR AGAINST THE MAFIA	P401	$1.25
————	# 2	DEATH SQUAD	P402	$1.25
————	# 3	BATTLE MASK	P403	$1.25
————	# 4	MIAMI MASSACRE	P404	$1.25
————	# 5	CONTINENTAL CONTRACT	P405	$1.25
————	# 6	ASSAULT ON SOHO	P406	$1.25
————	# 7	NIGHTMARE IN NEW YORK	P407	$1.25
————	# 8	CHICAGO WIPEOUT	P408	$1.25
————	# 9	VEGAS VENDETTA	P409	$1.25
————	#10	CARIBBEAN KILL	P410	$1.25
————	#11	CALIFORNIA HIT	P411	$1.25
————	#12	BOSTON BLITZ	P412	$1.25
————	#13	WASHINGTON I.O.U.	P413	$1.25
————	#14	SAN DIEGO SIEGE	P414	$1.25
————	#15	PANIC IN PHILLY	P415	$1.25
————	#16	SICILIAN SLAUGHTER	P416	$1.25
————	#17	JERSEY GUNS	P417	$1.25
————	#18	TEXAS STORM	P418	$1.25
————	#19	DETROIT DEATHWATCH	P419	$1.25
————	#20	NEW ORLEANS KNOCKOUT	P475	$1.25
————	#21	FIREBASE SEATTLE	P499	$1.25
————	#22	HAWAIIAN HELLGROUND	P625	$1.25

TO ORDER   AND MORE TO COME . . .

Please check the space next to the book/s you want, send this order form together with your check or money order, include the price of the book/s and 25¢ for handling and mailing to:

PINNACLE BOOKS, INC. / P.O. Box 4347
Grand Central Station / New York, N.Y. 10017

☐ **CHECK HERE IF YOU WANT A FREE CATALOG**

I have enclosed $————————check————————or money order————————
as payment in full. No C.O.D.'s

Name————————————————————————————————

Address——————————————————————————————

City————————————State————————Zip————————
(Please allow time for delivery)

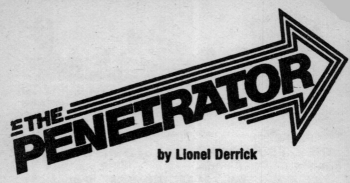